THE GARDENER'S SECRET AND OTHER STORIES

BY
CHARLES D. PATTON
2025

NOTICE

The Carvel Reynes Mysteries and Other Stories
© 2025 Applied Market Solutions, LLC

Some stories in this collection were originally published under the title *Ear Bug*. All have been significantly revised and re-edited for this edition.

Because these stories are primarily set in historical or earlier time periods, gender references and inclusive language reflect the context of those eras and may be limited by design.

Published by:
Short Mystery Press

ISBN: 978-1-963809-35-0 (print and ebook editions)

Written for and sponsored by:
Applied Market Solutions, LLC
6045 Lexington Park
Orlando, FL 32819

Cover design: Book Design Company
Editor: Marsha Zinberg

Inspired by the works of Arthur Conan Doyle, Mark Twain, and Edgar Allan Poe.

4

CONTENTS

THE GARDENER'S SECRET
A Carvel Reynes Mystery

London – June 1915

I remember the day trouble first found our garden. The air was still, the roses in bloom, and I was halfway through a glass of brandy when the bell-pull rang—a sharp, metallic cry that shattered the calm.

Carvel Reynes looked up from his chair. Even at rest, the man radiated purpose; a detective's mind rarely idles. "Expecting anyone, Colonel?" he asked.

"I was hoping for no one," I said, rising. But I already knew the peace was over. When Carvel's name traveled ahead of him, it seldom brought social callers.

A thick-set man waited at the gate, his face shadowed beneath a miner's cap, the smell of earth and sweat clinging to him. "I've come to see Mr. Reynes," he said, eyes darting past me into the garden.

"Colonel Gordon Forster," I replied, stepping aside. "And you are?"

"Not important," he muttered and brushed past me.

Reynes rose to meet him. "Cornwall," he said. "A stannous worker, by the dust on your boots."

The man stopped. "How would you know that?"

"Tin leaves its mark," Reynes said mildly. "So does trouble. Why are you here?"

"Lord Hughes of Devon sent me. Says you're to come to Powderham Castle. Someone's gone missing."

Reynes studied him for a moment, then smiled faintly. "Two hundred miles for a disappearance. That's never a simple case."

The messenger turned and left without another word.

Reynes watched him go, then glanced at me. "Well, Colonel—for once, shall we chase the storm instead of waiting for it?"

I drained the rest of my brandy. "At dawn, then."

As I bowed in greeting, I noticed the gardener trimming hedges nearby. He seemed more absorbed in plucking leaves than acknowledging our arrival, and I noticed him stagger slightly. From the corner of my eye, I saw Reynes observing him too.

"Allow me to show you to your rooms," the earl said. "On the way, I'll explain what brought you here."

As we climbed the castle's grand staircase, our footsteps echoed beneath carved archways and ancestral portraits. Lord Hughes began his tale without preamble.

"Roughly a month ago," he said, "my grandson's tutor, Dr. Chesterton, discovered a skeleton in a limestone cave near Cheddar Village. At first, we feared it might be our son, William, who vanished without a trace two years ago. But Chesterton quickly determined that the remains were far older, ancient, in fact. He believed it might be one of the oldest ever found in England."

Reynes and I exchanged a glance. My military instincts tingled. Disappearances and buried bones rarely made comfortable bedfellows.

"I asked the constable to secure the site," the earl continued. "But by the time he arrived, the skeleton, and several primitive stone tools discovered alongside it, had been stolen. Dr. Chesterton was devastated. I summoned you, Mr. Reynes, to find out who took it and why. The tutor's grief is now interfering with his role here. My grandson must be prepared to inherit this estate, and Chesterton's mind is elsewhere."

Reynes nodded. "We'll visit the cave at first light."

"Thank you. You must be tired from your long ride. Dinner will be sent to your rooms, and I'll have a lunch basket prepared for tomorrow."

He left us at adjoining chambers, heavy with brocade and the scent of lavender soap. As I changed from travel clothes, I found myself already turning over the details in my mind. A vanished skeleton. A distracted tutor. And a family with a missing heir.

The next morning, we met Constable Fitzgerald in Cheddar Village. He was a compact, red-haired Irishman with the bearing of a man used to getting to the point.

"This way, gentlemen," he said, leading us on foot toward the hillside.

A narrow gap in the rock face opened into a shallow cavern. We ducked inside, guided by the flicker of the constable's torch. The space had been disturbed, evidence of recent digging, though now empty.

Fitzgerald crouched near a pile of loose stone. "Chesterton said the skeleton was curled in a fetal position, surrounded by half a dozen flint tools. He believed it was over ten thousand years old."

"Who else knew of the discovery?" Reynes asked.

"Just Chesterton, his wife, and myself. I posted a guard the moment I could, but by then it was gone. I did spot a man leaving the area the day before I arrived, a thin fellow, about six foot tall, grey hair, moving quickly. I only saw him from behind."

We thanked the constable and made the return journey in silence. Reynes was already piecing something together, I could see it in his eyes.

That evening, dressed for dinner, we joined the earl, and an array of guests gathered near the dining room.

"Ah, Mr. Reynes, Colonel Forster," the earl said. "Allow me to introduce my financial advisor, Sir Willard Parsons." Parsons was wiry, his suit draped like a loose skin on a scarecrow frame.

"And this couple is Dr. John Chesterton and his wife Beatrice," the earl continued. "Dr. Chesterton, as you know, is my grandson's tutor."

Chesterton had the look of a worn cardigan, slumped posture, wrinkled suit, and sagging cheeks. His wife was prim, dressed in black with a lace shawl pinned by a pink pearl cameo.

Reynes extended his hand. "We visited the cave this morning. A curious site."

"Yes," Chesterton sighed. "That skeleton could've been the find of a lifetime. It would've restored everything, my work, my name…"

"You're being too modest," Beatrice said, patting his arm. "Willard was a professor at Oxford."

The maid entered quietly. "Dinner is served."

As we took our seats, Elizabeth and young Charles arrived, followed by a last-minute guest.

"Professor Roberts," the butler announced.

A tall man with a hooked nose and greying hair entered, his sharp eyes scanning the table. When he spotted Chesterton, a visible jolt passed between them. The tension thickened.

"I met Professor Roberts last week at the Bays Farmhouse pub," the earl said. "He's quite knowledgeable on anthropology. I invited him to share a few insights about early Devon settlers, how timely it turned out to be."

Two more introductions followed: Dr. Treacle, the family physician, and Mr. Pembroke, a young man in a crisp suit who positioned himself between Elizabeth and her son.

"Elizabeth's fiancé," the earl said. "He's been a welcome addition to the household."

The meal passed in pleasant enough conversation, Devon's mining history, railway investments, and the young doctor's ambitions, but beneath the surface, tensions simmered.

After dinner, the men moved to the study for brandy. The room was warm with polished wood, a suit of armor, and trophies of bygone hunts. Elizabeth soon joined us. The mood had only just begun to settle when young Charles burst in.

"Momma, come quick! Something's wrong with Mr. McDougal, in the greenhouse!"

We rushed along the garden path behind young Charles, who led us to the greenhouse. The evening air had turned chill, but the greenhouse glowed with residual warmth from the day's sun and smoldering heat from a nearby refuse pile.

Inside, we found Jack McDougal, shirtless, facedown between rows of orchids, limbs twisted unnaturally.

Reynes knelt and gently rolled the man over. Dr. Treacle was already beside him, checking for signs of life.

"Dead," the physician said grimly. "No visible wounds, but his face shows pain, perhaps intense pain."

He leaned in close, sniffed. "No almond odor. So, not cyanide, possibly arsenic. It's a byproduct of tin mining."

"I'll run tests after the autopsy," he added.

Reynes turned to a shelf of gardening supplies, inspecting each container. "Fertilizers, soil additives… nothing overtly suspicious," he muttered. Then he picked up an empty glass from a nearby bench. "No fingerprints," he noted, handing it to the doctor. "Best include this in your tests."

He crossed to a rustic desk and rifled through drawers. In the back of one, hidden beneath a logbook, he found a thin stack of pound notes.

"Curious," Reynes said, tucking the ledger beneath his arm.

Outside, the household stood huddled in silence, Lady Hughes pale, Elizabeth holding Charles close, the maid sniffling.

"Did anyone see anything unusual today?" Reynes asked.

There was a pause until the cook spoke up.

"I saw cherry pits in the kitchen dustbin. Odd. I'm the only one who usually discards there."

Reynes nodded. "Indeed."

He paused near a pile of still-warm ashes beside the greenhouse. He crouched, poking the embers with a stick. Something caught his eye. He fished out a scrap of scorched cloth and slipped it into his coat pocket.

The earl remained with Dr. Treacle, sending his butler to fetch the constable. Reynes and I returned to the study with Elizabeth, Charles, her fiancé, Professor Roberts, Dr. Chesterton, and his wife. The mood was thick with unease.

Soon, Charles was ushered off to bed by the maid, leaving us adults to sit in low, tense conversation.

Reynes turned to the professor. "Tell me, what brings you to this dusty corner of England?"

"I'm studying Cheddar Wood," he replied. "Its dwarf-shrub heath is remarkable."

"Ah, a botanist," I said. "Any archaeological interest?"

The professor hesitated, glancing at the Chestertons. "Nothing to speak of."

Beatrice stood abruptly. "Excuse me," she said, and left. Her husband followed.

"Do you believe McDougal was murdered?" Pembroke asked.

"I do," Reynes said plainly.

"But why?" he asked.

"That's what we aim to discover."

I held back the question on my mind, was the gardener's death connected to the missing skeleton? The answer, I suspected, was yes.

Morning broke with a fog rolling low over the castle lawn. Reynes and I sat on the rear veranda, tea and toast before us, as a tired but determined Dr. Treacle approached.

"I worked through the night," he said, dropping a folded report on the table. "You were right. The poison was cyanide, not arsenic. I don't know why I couldn't smell it, perhaps I'm one of those who can't. This was my first poisoning."

Reynes offered a polite nod. "Thank you, Doctor. Go get some rest."

Treacle nodded and departed. Reynes skimmed the report, then turned back to the logbook.

"I deciphered it last night," he said. "The entries are financial, dates, initials, and pound amounts."

"Blackmail, then?" I asked.

"Almost certainly. Larger sums than a gardener could earn honestly. Debits from E.H., credits to J.L., and later, payments from W.P."

"E.H. must be Elizabeth Hughes. W.P. is Willard Parsons. And J.L., the maid?"

"Possibly. Jenny Lowry. Let's see what she knows."

As if summoned, Jenny appeared to collect the breakfast dishes.

"Jenny," Reynes said, "may we ask you a few questions?"

She blinked but nodded. We offered her a seat; she remained standing.

"Your last name?" he asked.

"Lowry."

"You were receiving money from Jack McDougal. Was it blackmail?"

Her face flushed. "No, sir. He loved me. He gave me money to help with savings."

"You may not have poisoned him," I said, "but you're withholding evidence. That makes you a suspect."

Her shoulders slumped. "All right. It wasn't my idea. Two years ago, I walked into the study and caught Miss Elizabeth altering numbers in Sir Parsons' ledgers. She didn't see me, but I saw the panic on her face."

"You told Jack," Reynes guessed.

She nodded. "I snuck him in later. He could read accounts better than I. He figured out she was embezzling. Thousands of pounds."

"Why steal from her own father?" I asked.

"Her brother William was set to inherit everything. She knew if he did, she'd get nothing. So she helped herself while she could."

"And when William disappeared?" I asked.

"She was ill that week, laid up in the infirmary," she said quickly. "Couldn't have done it."

"She had no need to steal after that," I said. "And she met Mr. Pembroke, who must have convinced her to stop."

Reynes stepped into a shaft of light, pacing slowly.

"So Jack turned his sights on Parsons next," he said. "Blamed him for not catching the fraud. That explains the later entries."

We dismissed Jenny and waited until she was out of earshot.

"That clears her," Reynes said. "And likely Elizabeth. But the timing of the murder is telling. All the men were together in the study."

"So the poison must have been delivered by a woman," I said.

Reynes nodded. "That leaves Lady Hughes or Mrs. Chesterton. And poison is often a woman's weapon."

The next morning dawned grey and damp, a light mist hanging over Powderham's hedgerows. We took breakfast in silence, the weight of the previous night's revelations still heavy in the air.

I finally broke the quiet. "How did the gardener find Professor Roberts to begin with?"

Reynes sipped his tea, then replied, "He sent a telegram to the university, seeking an anthropologist. By chance, the message reached Roberts. Likely intercepted and answered before anyone else saw it."

"And McDougal, not knowing the professor's history with the Chestertons, thought nothing of it."

"Exactly. He was paid for the tip, then tried to sell the same information back to the Chestertons, thinking he could play both sides."

"The wickedest kind of luck for them all," I muttered. "And what of the missing heir, William?"

Reynes stood and looked out across the lawn, where Charles was playing with a small wooden sword beneath the watchful eye of the butler.

"We'll begin that search when we're back in London," he said. "Something tells me the Earl hasn't told us everything."

I nodded slowly. "What a thing, for a single skeleton to unravel so many secrets."

"History has a habit of doing that," Reynes said. "Dig deep enough, and you don't just find bones, you find motives, grudges, and truths people hoped would stay buried."

As the countryside rolled by, I glanced at my companion, always calm, always observing.

"How did you know it wasn't the professor who murdered the gardener?" I asked.

"I didn't," Reynes said. "Not at first. But the timing of the poisoning, the manner of death, it all pointed to someone close. And grief can turn to vengeance with frightening ease."

The wheels of the carriage rattled louder as we reached a stone bridge.

I turned to the window and smiled faintly. "Where shall we go next, Reynes?"

He gave the smallest shrug. "Wherever the next bell-pull rings."

THE IVORY VENGEANCE

A Carvel Reynes Mystery

London -- 1916

I was about to knock on the apartment door of my friend, Mr. Carvel Reynes, when the door suddenly flew open.

"Colonel, Scotland Yard beckons," Reynes said, locking the door behind him with haste. "Would you care to accompany me?"

His reputation as a private detective was fast ascending, ever since the *London Times* praised his uncanny knack for unraveling mysteries from the slimmest of clues. Through our friendship, and perhaps owing to my military discipline, Reynes sometimes invited me to assist him in his inquiries. Of course, I agreed at once. I followed him through the hall as nimbly as my damaged leg permitted. In minutes, we were down the stairs and into a Hansom cab, headed through the drizzle toward Scotland Yard.

At Number 4 Whitehall Place, we had no sooner crossed the threshold than a familiar voice called out: "Reynes! Colonel Forster!"

It was Inspector Warren Nelson, a long-past acquaintance from my military days and now a tenured fixture at the Yard. He looked much the same as he had during the Crimean campaign, though his potbelly now tugged at the buttons of his coat.

"Colonel," he said, shaking my hand warmly, "by God, you've still got that cavalry spine. Still favoring the leg?"

"Glad to have what's left of it," I replied.

Carvel gave me a curious glance, my wounding at Balaclava had not come up between us before.

"Gentlemen," Nelson said, ushering us into his cramped, dingy office, "we have a problem."

"A series of murders," he began. "Three titled men, all in the last three days. Each found dead in his bed, killed by a single upward thrust with a long, curved blade. Straight through the lower rib cage and into the heart."

"Efficient and deliberate," said Reynes. "What were their names?"

"Lord Chester of Shropshire. Sir Robert Latchford, Fourth Earl of Norfolk. And Arthur Wellman, Duke of Sherwood."

"Three peers?" I said. "Surely they ran in the same social circles."

"You'd think so," said Nelson. "But we've found no links, none. Latchford was an eccentric farmer. The Duke dealt in lumber. Chester was a House peer. No correspondence, no shared ventures, not even a common club. No signs of forced entry, no valuables missing."

Reynes began pacing. "Either they knew their killer... or the killer is unusually skilled at remaining unseen."

"Exactly," said Nelson. "And the Commissioner is feeling heat from Parliament. We could use your help, both of you."

"You have it," said Reynes. "We'll start with the crime scenes."

In the days that followed, Reynes and I toured all three estates. Each was remote, affluent, and, to my surprise, oddly solitary.

Lord Chester's estate was a monument to big-game hunting: mounted African trophies, elephant-foot stools, chairs fashioned from tusks. French doors at the rear of the house were left unlatched. His Basenji dogs, prized for their quiet yodels rather than barks, had been kenneled some distance away. No witnesses, no signs of struggle.

Sir Robert Latchford's farm was modest in scale but sprawling in passion, ribbons from livestock fairs adorned every wall. The house smelled of hay and lavender oil. We found a large Australian cattle dog, silenced with the same lethal precision as his master. His study held cages of hedgehogs and a curious collection of cowry shells. Odd. But again, no obvious leads.

The Duke of Sherwood lived adjacent to the legendary forest. His estate was rich with rare hardwood furnishings, ebony, teak, bubinga. He was a conservationist at heart, with no security animals. His murder, like the others, had left no trace.

At each home, we found nothing stolen, no evidence of a break-in, and no helpful observations from staff. The only commonality seemed to be solitude: all three were single, childless, and exceedingly wealthy.

Back in London, Reynes invited me to his apartment for tea and reflection.

"Well, Colonel?" he asked. "What binds these men together?"

"Beyond affluence and isolation... nothing."

"Exactly," he said, pouring tea. "Nothing we saw. Which means the link lies in what we haven't seen. Their finances."

"I'll investigate their heirs," I offered. "Perhaps we'll find a common banker."

"Do," said Reynes. "While you do that, I shall consult Professor Weatherly at Oxford on a parallel matter."

"On what matter?" I asked.

"You'll know in due time."

With that, he returned to his notes. His urgency was palpable.

The next morning, I returned to Baker Street with news.

"All three men banked with Parson-Beckman in Whitehall."

Reynes smiled. "Excellent. Professor Weatherly, by the way, is an expert in Eastern Hemisphere trade. He provided an insight or two I'll explain shortly. But first, let's visit our banker."

At Parson-Beckman, we were shown into the office of Gilbert Parson himself, a mousey, sharp-featured man in an elegant Savile Row suit, wearing arrogance like a cravat.

"Sir," Reynes said smoothly, "we're investigating the recent murders of three of your clients. Might they have been partners in any venture?"

"We do not discuss clients' affairs," Parson said with a sneer.

I bristled. "Scotland Yard may take a different view if delays in your cooperation lead to further deaths."

Parson paled. "Very well. All I can say is this, there was a shipment. Ivory. Arrived last week from India. And something went missing."

"Thank you," said Reynes. "That's all we need for now."

We went to see Nelson at once.

"A cargo ship docked last week," he confirmed. "Missing crates of carved ivory. Captain says it vanished during a storm, no other ships in the area. No suspects."

"We need to speak with that captain," Reynes said.

And off we went again.

We found *The Star of Bombay* docked near the Port of London. Its iron hull showed patches of rust, and the scent of salt and tar hung in the damp air. The captain, a wiry red-haired man in a tidy navy coat, greeted us at the gangway.

"Captain," Reynes began, "I am Carvel Reynes, and this is Colonel Forster. We're investigating a case that may involve your last cargo. Specifically, the missing ivory."

The captain exhaled. "Yes, a strange matter. We were sailing near the Portuguese coast in heavy weather. I had personally inspected the lashings on the ivory before the worst of the storm. Upon arriving in London, we discovered the crates were empty. No signs of forced entry. No other vessels near us."

"What else did you carry?" I asked.

"Bolts of printed silk, rough-cut sandalwood planks, and a small consignment of gold jewelry, secured and untouched. Only the sandalwood was disturbed, bindings snapped during the storm."

"May we see the hold?" asked Reynes.

"Of course."

Below deck, we found the sandalwood strewn about in messy piles. The empty ivory crates were stacked neatly along one wall.

"Your crew left those crates like that?" Reynes asked.

"No," the captain replied. "That's how we found them."

"Interesting," Reynes murmured.

The captain continued. "The ivory shipment was large, over six hundred carvings. Some entire tusks. All gone."

"And yet your gold was untouched," I said.

"Precisely."

"And the crew?" Reynes asked.

"My first mate is Njenga, a Mijikenda man from Kenya. Formerly a tribal leader, I've heard. Brilliant sailor. The rest are a mix; Portuguese, Africans, and Taiwanese, hired across various ports. Njenga's the linchpin, respected, multilingual, capable."

"Would you mind if we looked around?" Reynes asked.

"Not at all."

Reynes explored every corner of the hold, tapping bulkheads, checking ceiling joints, and inspecting containers. I followed him as best I could, my cane thudding on the boards.

"What do you think?" I asked. "Was it sabotage? Theft?"

"If it were profit-motivated," he said, "they'd sell it. But what if the motive wasn't profit?"

"Spite?"

"Possibly. Or something more personal."

"What about balloons?" I asked. "Some say heavy items can be lifted and flown."

"In storm winds?" he said, shaking his head. "No. But the sandalwood, something's off."

He turned back toward the hold and carefully examined the wood as crewmen restacked it.

"Why sandalwood?" I asked. "It's so dense it barely floats."

"Exactly," said Reynes. He paused, bent down, and picked up a thin, splintered shard from beneath the wood. "This isn't sandalwood. It's pine."

He tapped it against my palm. It was featherlight.

"If they packed the ivory atop pine pallets, then during the storm…"

"…they could float the crates out through a hatch," I said, suddenly understanding. "Slip them into the sea and let the current carry them."

"Brilliant," he said. "Now, the question is: who did it, and why?"

We returned to the ship the next morning before it sailed. The dockhands were loading new cargo. At Reynes's request, the captain assembled his crew.

"I believe I've solved your mystery," Reynes began. "The ivory was set afloat, on pine pallets, beneath the sandalwood. It was deliberate."

The crew murmured. Njenga stood still, arms crossed.

"And the motive wasn't money," Reynes said. "The ivory wasn't sold, it was sent home."

"To Africa," I added.

Njenga stepped forward, his voice even but firm.

"Aye. I did it."

"Alone?" Reynes asked.

A few crewmen nodded, but Njenga raised a hand.

"No. Only me. My idea. My doing."

He looked at the captain, not defiant, but proud.

Reynes studied him.

"You knew the financiers were the same three men who died."

"I followed the bank's agent from this ship to his office," Njenga said. "Then I saw the rich man visit. I heard names shouted, three men who funded the theft of my people."

"Not just ivory, then," I said.

"No," said Njenga. "Slaves. Years ago. Those men funded the trade. One we caught... he told us. Then he died."

Njenga stepped back. "I joined this crew. I came here. I waited. And I avenged them."

The captain looked conflicted but said nothing.

Reynes turned, stepped onto the gangway, then looked back.

"I'll be informing the Yard," he said. "Tomorrow morning. Around nine."

I followed, but not before noting the shared glance between captain and first mate. The captain's shoulders softened, and Njenga nodded once, grateful, perhaps, or simply at peace.

Back at the apartment, Reynes poured brandy.

"Justice," I said, "wears many faces."

"And not all wear wigs," he replied.

"How did you know they were in the slave trade?"

"The cowry shells were the first clue, African currency. Then something Parson said: '...one of our ships.' A fleet, then. The rest was context. And Weatherly confirmed the ivory was just a veneer, slavery ran deeper."

"And Njenga?" I asked.

"A man with many talents," Reynes said. "Including patience."

After our final conversation over brandy, Reynes sank into his chair, fingers laced in thought.

"What became of Njenga," I asked, "after we walked away?"

"He returned to his duties, I presume," Reynes said. "The captain's silence was its own verdict."

"You think he'll face no justice?"

Reynes looked at me over the rim of his glass. "Justice came and went, delivered by Njenga, endorsed by history, and permitted by us."

"I'm not sure I could have done the same," I said.

"No," Reynes replied. "That's why he had to."

He stood and moved to the window. Outside, London gas lamps flickered in the mist. Somewhere beyond them, the ship was already gone, fading toward Africa, and perhaps toward a reckoning deeper than courts could hold.

"Colonel," Reynes said, "Some mysteries end in trials. Others in understanding. This was the latter."

I nodded. I felt the ache in my old leg, a reminder of a war long past, and thought of the long pain others had carried silently.

29

"Will we see Njenga again?" I asked.

"I doubt it," Reynes said. "But I believe he's already home."

THE SHADOW ON RANDOLPH STREET
A Carvel Reynes Mystery

London -- 1917

On a warm spring afternoon, Reynes and I were sitting and sipping brandies at a sidewalk table at Chez Victor's café on Wardour Street in Piccadilly. As we were talking, I noticed a well-dressed senorita with regal comportment walking toward our table. I sensed from the determination in her stride that she was headed straight for Reynes.

Reynes had recently been subjected to extensive newspaper publicity after solving a high-profile case, where he recovered a jeweled crown stolen from one of Britain's revered princesses. Now, odd strangers were appearing out of nowhere wanting to hire him. I was hoping this lady was not another. I had already cautioned him several times to be selective in choosing new cases, because he could just as easily reverse his burgeoning reputation with a couple of publicized failures. He ignored my advice.

As she arrived at our table, being middle-aged gentlemen with manners, we rose from our chairs as we would for any woman, but perhaps a little more gingerly for a young, attractive one. As she was six foot tall and thin, she towered over Reynes, with his short and stocky build. For that matter, even though I am a good six inches taller than Reynes, she overshadowed me by a few inches as well. Her dark brown hair matched her eyes. She wore a small black pillbox hat tilted at a jaunty angle, its short veil draped over the top of her forehead. She radiated Spanish gentility. Reynes motioned for her to sit down and join us at our table. As she did, I could faintly smell the aroma of a fine perfume. Forgetting I had set my bowler on

31

that chair, I managed to snatch it up an instant before she sat on it. She was so focused on Reynes that she didn't even notice my rapid retrieval.

"Excuse me for doing my own introduction, but I feel I have no time to arrange a proper one," she said with a light Spanish accent. "I am Senorita Antonia Montilla Alvarez de Castile."

"This is Mr. Carvel Reynes, and I am Colonel Gordon Forster, his assistant," I replied.

"I am familiar with your reputations," Senorita Montilla said. "That is why I came."

"How might we assist?" Reynes asked.

"I am deeply concerned about my fiancé, Jerome Staunton," she said. "I believe his army service ended, but he has not returned to me yet. It would be completely out of character for him not to return or not to let me know if he has been delayed."

She pulled a letter from her handbag. "Here is his last letter, in which he wrote that he would be mustered out in April. Money is no object. I need you to find him or find out what happened to him."

"Where was he posted?" I asked.

"India," she replied. "He was a lieutenant in the 18th Royal Irish, 2ND battalion."

"Can you describe him, please," I asked next.

"He is tall, six foot three, with red hair, and missing the smallest finger on his left hand, lost in a skirmish with the Sapoys during their rebellion."

"Have you gone to the police about this matter?" Reynes asked.

She sighed. "I tried. But the desk sergeant dismissed me summarily because he said no crime had been committed and they didn't intervene in lovers' spats in the absence of violence."

Reynes went silent for a minute, then gave her a long look before saying, "We will make some inquiries and see what we can learn. "

The slightest smile crossed her lips. "Thank you. I am deeply worried." She paused for an instant. "Here is my card. Please let me know the moment you learn anything."

With that, she rose and seemingly glided away.

The next morning was rainy and, as agreed the evening before, I met Reynes at the Office of Military Records. After making some inquiries, we learned that Lt. Staunton had been discharged in April as he expected. We were able to obtain the address he had left the army to send his final pay, 107 Randolph Street. We left the building and didn't speak until we reached the street.

"We should proceed with caution until we know what we are dealing with," Reynes said. "I will do a preliminary survey of the address and then meet you later. In the meantime, to confirm or deny the possibility of his death, please visit the Department of Vital Statistics and see if they have a death certificate on file for Mr. Jerome Staunton."

I did as Reynes requested, found no such record, and then returned to my apartment.

That afternoon, it had turned drizzly. Responding to a loud knock, I opened my door expecting Reynes. To my surprise, standing before me was a rough-looking seaman dressed in a dark blue coat, oily pants, and knit hat. His clothes were wet, worn, and ragged, his face dirty, and his black beard, sideburns, and hair matted from the rain.

"Sir, I am unwilling to accept beggars at my door," I said. "As you can understand -- for otherwise a queue would form down the hallway and out into the street. My apologies."

As I began to close the door, the man stuck his foot in the opening to stop me. My temper flared and I raised my fists, prepared to defend myself.

"Hold on," he said, holding up his hands.

To my shock, the ruffian pulled off his beard, wig, and even fake sideburns, revealing my colleague, Mr. Reynes. He came in and sat down.

"Why are you in disguise?" I asked. "I've never known you to resort to such subterfuge."

"I reasoned that if Mr. Staunton was residing at the house and had not contacted his fiancé that he might be held against his will or possibly hiding," Reynes said. "Being unsure of the circumstances, along with the potential of being recognized by any of the city's criminal elements and now by countless average citizens, I wanted to blend into the surroundings. Staying close to the docks, I thought I could become nearly invisible by dressing as a common seaman , a class of workers many people in the area were likely to look right past, and I was right."

"What did you discover?" I asked.

"The unexpected," Reynes said. "Staunton is the man living at that address. A street urchin told me the house was a rental property and was able to describe the man living there. The boy's description matched the one Senorita Montilla gave us , including the missing finger.

"That's not entirely unexpected," I said.

"True," Reynes said. "Unexpected was the woman I saw looking out of an upstairs window. Mr. Staunton may have another woman in his life. However, she was unusually muscular, which struck me as an odd match for a gentleman. Further, I also saw two sinister-looking Chinese thugs lurking in the lane behind his house. They seemed to be watching the house but not approaching it , yet."

"What does their presence mean and what will we tell Senorita Montilla?" I asked.

"I already stopped at her house on my way here. She was indisposed in her boudoir at the time so I sent a note to her through her maid, advising of my belief that Mr. Staunton was alive, giving her the specifics on his current whereabouts and letting her know that an unknown woman may also be in the house. She sent back a reply that she would sleep on the news overnight and send word in the morning with directions for our next steps."

"Then, we must await her word," I said.

The next morning, I was again awakened by pounding on my front door. Reynes came in waving a newspaper.

"Look at this," he said.

He showed me the headlines on the Times. It said, "Man found murdered at 107 Randolph Street."

"Is it Staunton?" I asked.

"Yes," Reynes said. "I went directly to see Senorita Montilla, but she was gone."

"Do you mean temporarily or permanently?" I asked.

"Gone, moved with no forwarding address," he said. "I also went to Randolph Street and found no sign of the other woman or the Chinese thugs. The only clue I found was a piece of paper blowing along the front porch." He handed me the paper. The note read "Scarper the Taber. Black Dogs here. Gone for minger." It was signed, "Your favorite Voltige."

"What language is that?" I asked.

"It is vaguely familiar to me, but I can't put my finger on it." Reynes said.

"How odd this case has become -- seems this case has shifted from finding the senorita's fiancé to finding some combination of up to three suspects in his murder," I said. "Where do we start?"

"First, we have an obligation to report Senorita Montilla to Scotland Yard, as they are unaware that she could be a suspect," he said.

We left to make the report.

In the process of delivering our report to Scotland Yard's Captain Wilson, we learned that Mr. Staunton had been under suspicion for having stolen and likely hidden a large army payroll just before he was discharged. The Yard had identified that one of Staunton's army mates was Johnny Wong, son of the leader of a notorious Chinese gang called the Black Dogs. Staunton was found lying on his back with his body bruised and battered. According to the coroner, on first inspection, the body wounds did not appear to have been the cause of his death. An autopsy would be completed in the next day or two to identify the cause of death.

Leaving the Yard, Reynes said, "If Staunton stole the money, he may have made the mistake of confiding in the wrong person, Johnny Wong. That would explain the gangsters lurking behind the house."

"Further investigation could be dangerous," I said.

"We still have work to do," Reynes said. "Let's return to the scene of the crime."

As we turned onto Randolph Street, Reynes stopped cold in front of the side wall of a pub and stared at a poster advertising a traveling circus.

"Why does that poster so fascinate you?" I asked.

"It tells me where to find the muscular woman," Reynes said.

"How does it tell you that?" I asked.

"It melds two bits of information for us," he said. "I remember what the language was on the note. It was Parlari, the language of circus performers. The muscular woman I saw in the window is probably a circus performer. We must leave for the circus now, before they pull up stakes and move to their next town."

In forty-five minutes, we arrived at the circus. We asked every performer we could find about the muscular woman, but true to form for circus people, they would tell us nothing about one of their own. Only after locating the manager and satisfying him that we were not the police did he take us to a small, colorfully painted, wooden-wheeled Gypsy wagon. Knocking on the door at the back of the wagon, a woman appeared in full-body tights that left bare her muscular arms, which were covered with tattoos of snakes, flowers, and hearts. Her name was simply Rosy.

"Rosy, were you in a house with a Mr. Staunton on Randolph street yesterday?" Reynes asked.

She just stared at us.

"We are not inspectors from the Yard," I said. "We are private detectives working for Staunton's fiancé." My comment did little to lessen her reluctance.

"We need to know the exact nature of your relationship with Mr. Staunton," Reynes said. "If you don't help us, we will need to let Scotland Yard know you were there."

He began to pace.

"He hired me to be a stand-in for his fiancé," Rosy said. "To insulate her from some threats he had received. We slept in separate rooms, of course."

"Were you there when he was attacked?" I asked.

"No," she said. "I went to get food. As I was leaving, I saw two of the Black Dogs in the alley."

"How do you know the Black Dogs?" Reynes asked.

"Let's just say I learned about that gang from fellow circus performers," Rosy said. "They have a unique tattoo on their hands that I could see, even at a distance." She asked for a pen and paper, which I was able to provide. She drew these Chinese characters, 沮丧.

"The first character is on the back of their left hands," she explained. And the second on their rights. Together, in Chinese, the characters say Black Dogs."

"I am familiar with that gang, Reynes said.

"Why didn't you fetch the police?" I asked.

"I did," she said. "When I first left, Mr. Staunton locked the door behind me and returned to the top floor of the house. To not make him come back down, I hastily scribbled a note and dropped it through the mail slot. I wrote it in my circus lingo because I knew Staunton learned the language from his father, who had owned circuses."

"What did the note say, in plain English, if you would?" I asked.

"I told him to fly the coup as soon as possible, that Black Dogs were nearby, and that I was going for the police -- so he could tell them what he knew."

"I believe you signed it as your favorite Voltige," I said. "What does that mean?"

"Voltige means horseback rider," she said.

"How long before you returned to the house?" Reynes asked.

"It took me about thirty minutes to locate a bobby," she said. "When I returned, the front door was open, and Mr. Staunton was lying dead in the doorway of his first floor library."

"Did you see who did it?" I asked.

"No sign of anyone," Rosy said. "I split and came back here so I wouldn't become a suspect."

"While you were with him, when he was alive, did he say anything about stolen money?" Reynes asked.

"He did," she said. "He said some men might be coming after him about some stolen money that he had nothing to do with stealing," she said.

We thanked her for speaking with us and returned to our respective apartments.

The next day, Reynes and I attended Mr. Staunton's wake, the location of which we found in the newspaper obituaries. The service was held at a quaint country church just outside London towards Swindon. The wake was arranged by Staunton's aged parents and attended by them and a few other relatives. Laid out, he appeared as his fiancé had described -- tall, red hair, and missing a finger. We expected his fiancé to be among the grievers. We hoped to find her there so we could learn what she knew about Staunton's murder. But she did not attend, raising our suspicions about her.

"We have a mystery on our hands," I said. "We don't know what role the thugs played, and we have no inkling where the senorita has gone."

"The only way to find some daylight on this case is for me to visit Long Jiaboa," Reynes said.

"The leader of the Black Dogs?" I asked. Reynes nodded. "Want me to join you?"

"Better not," Reynes said. "Long Jiaboa can be unpredictable. I am hoping he will be willing to talk if I can get him to meet with me alone. I will visit him at the restaurant he runs this evening and rejoin you in the morning."

I met Reynes the next morning, after he had met the prior evening with the gang leader.

"Obviously, the gang leader let you return alive," I asked. "Did you learn anything helpful?"

"He spoke in metaphors, but I was able to conclude what he meant," Reynes said. He indicated that his men did not kill Staunton but beat him to extract information about the payroll. The beating was brief, only a few minutes, as a first warning. His men didn't kill Staunton. Jiaboa also indicated that they learned after the beating who did steal the payroll, and the thief was not Staunton."

"Our suspects are down to one and we don't know where Senorita Montilla is or why she would have killed her fiancé," I said.

Reynes pondered the questions. "If she was going to flee, where would she go?" he asked.

"She appeared to be Spanish," I said. "Perhaps Spain."

"Spain is not far enough," he said. "Maybe South America."

"In either event, she would have to travel by ship," I said.

"Grab a Times and let's check ship departures," he said.

I ran to the corner for a newspaper and returned in minutes. I promptly found the table of ship departure times.

"The first ship to depart for South America from the Port of London since the murder was The Santiago," I said. "The ship is scheduled to depart at 10:00 PM this evening for Argentina.

"We must hurry to the ship now," Reynes said. "I will go ahead. You rush over to the Yard and get Captain Wilson and four of his men and bring them to the ship."

Reynes arrived first at the ship, about a half hour before scheduled departure, and spoke with the captain. The captain showed Reynes the passenger list, and on that list, Reynes found only one woman traveling unaccompanied -- under the name of Srta. Carmen Marisol. I arrived minutes later with Captain Wilson and his men, just as the ship's captain was leading Reynes to the woman's cabin. Before knocking, Reynes took the inspector aside for a brief discussion and then returned and knocked. When she opened the door, we could see that Senorita Marisol was Senorita Montilla.

"What have you to say?" Reynes asked.

"Come in," she said. "How may I help you?"

"Tell us how and why you killed your fiancé," Reynes said.

"That's preposterous," she said. "Just because I couldn't stand to attend his funeral doesn't mean I didn't love him."

"You may have loved him once, but you did kill him," Reynes said.

"How could you say that?" she asked.

"Because I was just informed that the autopsy shows he was killed by a puncture through his ear and into his brain, with a long, thin object such as a hat pin," he said. "A hat pin is a favorite murder weapon for women."

"Yes, women," she said. "You should look for that powerfully built woman who was staying with him."

"A circus performer is unlikely to wear a fashionable hat that requires a hat pin," Reynes said. "Certainly not as fancy a hat pin as the one that was holding your hat in place when you first came to visit the colonel and me. You also just revealed a key piece of evidence. You must have seen the woman yourself to know she was muscular because I did not include that information in the note that I sent up to you."

This observation flustered the senorita.

"Let me tell you what happened," Reynes said. "On the morning after I left you the note, you went to the house where Staunton was living to see for yourself that he was living with another woman. You watched the house until you saw the woman leave. Before you could approach the house, you saw the two gang members enter the house and start beating your fiancé. You could see through the open front door and felt he was getting the punishment he deserved for leaving you. You then began screaming to scare off the thugs. The moment the gangsters left, you entered the house, found him in the library doorway lying on the floor, dazed from the beating, and used that opportunity to stick your hat pin into his brain, through his ear. You thought the cause of death would be blamed on the gangsters' beatings."

"You are guessing," she said. "You have no proof -- no hat pin, no witnesses."

"I suspect that you kept that hat pin and that we will find it among your belongings here in your cabin," Reynes said.

The inspector began to search and in minutes found her jewelry case and the hatpin.

"Still has blood on it," he said.

"What makes your crime particularly sad is that Mr. Staunton didn't leave you," Reynes said. "He hired the muscular woman, Rosy, to stand in for you -- to protect you from threats he was receiving from the Black Dogs gang because they had mistaken him for another person who stole a large military payroll. You killed your fiancé over a mistaken notion that he was cheating on you."

"No!" she screamed. "That isn't true! It can't be. Tell me it isn't!"

"It is true," Reynes said.

Looking at the inspector and me to confirm that the news was true, she suddenly jumped up and ran from the cabin before anyone could stop her. In a flash, she was at the ship's railing on the dock side. She threw herself over the railing and died grotesquely when her body met the solid surface of the loading dock below. Reynes and I ran after her, but we were too late and could do nothing other than watch. Unmistakably, one tragedy had resulted in another.

That evening, Reynes and I were back at Chez Victor's sidewalk café sipping brandies.

"How did you know the method by which Staunton was murdered?" I asked.

"My brief discussion with the inspector," Reynes said.

"The coroner identified the weapon as a hatpin?"

"No, the coroner simply confirmed that a thin object had pierced the victim's brain through the left ear," he said. "That told me it wasn't the Chinese. If they'd wanted him dead, they would've ended it with a blade to the heart, not something so surgical. I figured the killer was a woman. In cases like this, women usually resort to one of two weapons, poison, or if the man is defenseless, whatever sharp object is at hand. A knife. A hatpin."

"A woman scorned," I said. "An unfortunate outcome in this case."

"So true," he commented.

A Carvel Reynes Mystery

London -- 1918

I was sitting in my leather armchair reading the Sunday Herald when someone pounded loudly on my apartment door. When I opened it, before me stood young Billy Baldwin, a local Baker Street urchin.

"Colonel Forster, come quick," he hollered. "Mr. Reynes needs you."

Billy, a tow-headed lad about twelve years old, scruffy, and grimy, could often be found around Baker Street, begging or doing odd jobs for small sums. In the midst of his mumbled message, somewhat distorted by his street accent, I heard the word "murder," so grabbed my heavy tweed jacket and bowler and dashed off.

I arrived at 322 Baker Street in minutes, rushed up the stairs and through Reynes' open apartment door to find him sitting on the edge of his chair intently focused on, to my surprise, Mrs. Hudson. I knew Mrs. Hudson as Sherlock Holmes' landlady and from seeing her in the neighborhood.

Reynes wore a maroon smoking jacket and slippers. From his disheveled hair, I knew he must have been rousted by Mrs. Hudson as I had been by Billy. Since Holmes' disappearance, Reynes attempted to fill the void, picking-up odd cases now and again. Unlike Holmes in so many ways, Mr. Carvel Reynes was in his mid-fifties, short, solidly built, talkative, and jovial.

"Mrs. Hudson, this is Colonel Gordon Forster, my friend and confidant," Reynes said.

"How do you do?" she asked.

Mrs. Hudson, an older Scotswoman sporting grey hair tied in a bun, sat almost precariously on the edge of the settee while Reynes had pulled his wing chair up to sit closely in front of her.

"Colonel, Mrs. Hudson just advised me that a man's body lies crumpled on the floor in front of Sherlock Holmes apartment."

"While carrying a clothes basket to the attic, she actually stumbled over the body," Reynes said. "The man died in a contorted shape with a gruesome facial expression."

"Yes, as if death had silenced him in the middle of a scream," Mrs. Hudson said.

"I told Billy to alert Scotland Yard after he fetched you," Reynes said. "To give us time to inspect the crime scene before they disturb it."

"Did you say Holmes' apartment?" I asked.

"Yes," Mrs. Hudson said. "I've kept the apartment intact and locked. His rent was paid three years ahead and I've no desire to profit from his disappearance. Besides, his body was never recovered, so I still hold out faint hope."

She was clearly in denial.

"Understandable," Reynes said. "Let's go inspect the scene."

As we hurried towards Holmes' apartment, Reynes conversed with Mrs. Hudson to distract her from thinking about our destination.

"How did the man gain access to the second floor in the middle of the night?" Reynes asked.

"I must have forgotten to lock the street door," Mrs. Hudson said. "Even with the thin walls I heard no sound, but then I am a heavy sleeper. His look is ghastlier than anyone could imagine."

We soon arrived in front of the body, lying on the hallway floor directly in front of Holmes' apartment door. Just as Mrs. Hudson described, the body was wildly contorted, its limbs drawn up at different angles and the mouth locked open in a ghastly gape. Reynes knelt on one knee to inspect the body. The man's eyes were wide open until Reynes gently closed them. The man was young, in his mid-thirties, with a full head of black hair, wearing a dark-blue suit with high collar and ascot appropriate for a gentleman.

"Unusual rigor mortis," Reynes said.

He gently rocked the body back and forth to look beneath it. Near where the man's right hand had been, he positioned his right eye close to the floor. "Appears he drew the letter D on the floor in saliva," Reynes said. "Or, perhaps a P."

He searched the man's pockets. From the inside right pocket of the man's jacket, he withdrew a folded paper. Unfolding it exposed an unusual plant leaf with seven long, dark-green, narrow blades. He bent one slightly to find it dry but not brittle; informing him that the leaf was not old. He smelled the leaf where he had bent it and then refolded the leaf in the paper and slipped both into his inside jacket pocket. From the victim's left jacket pocket, Reynes extracted a small paper with a series of pinholes under a flap. He handed it to me. Inspecting it, I could make no sense of it, so I put it in my pocket.

Reynes inspected the man's neck, hair, hands, fingertips, and fingernails. Searching the man's watch pocket, he found a broken fingernail, unusually long, slender, and unpolished. He deposited the remnant in his handkerchief and slid it into his side pocket.

Then, he smelled the man's shirt cuff.

"No external signs of violence," he said. "Mrs. Hudson, you can return to your home. Colonel Forster will wait for the police. Colonel, ask the coroner to test for all known poisons; then come to find me at the new British Museum of Natural History, where we should learn the victim's name."

"How could you know that?" I asked.

"The small paper with holes, which I handed you, is used to hold straight pins favored by Entomologists to hold down insect specimens," he said. "And the man's shirt cuffs have a formaldehyde smell, a preservative used at such museums. My conclusion is not certain, but the museum seems a worthy place to start."

"I'll meet you at the managing director's office," I said.

Mr. Reynes and Mrs. Hudson departed.

In minutes, I heard the police ascending the stairs. Soon, as was relieved of guard duty.

I arrived at the managing director's office just as Reynes emerged. The director's name, Dr. Richard Owens, was painted on the door. A tall, thin, attractive blonde in a conservative grey uniform sat behind a secretary's desk in the lobby. I tipped my bowler to her, which she barely acknowledged. The name plate on her desk read Tatiana Demidova.

Reynes pulled me to the lobby's far end, whispering, "Colonel, the victim was Dr. Leonard Thompson, a botanist who returned two weeks ago from an exploration of West Africa, in French Guinea," Reynes said.

"I'm surprised a British citizen could operate in that country, given the tension between our government and the French," I said.

As we talked, Reynes was watching the secretary over my shoulder.

"What about the managing director?" I asked.

"Quite egocentric," Reynes said. "He said he's the leading biologist in the country and on the verge of becoming president of the Royal Society of Scientists, the most prestigious scientific society in London."

Reynes was still watching over my shoulder. So I started to look, but Reynes grabbed my wrist as a signal not to turn my head.

"His office was decorated with antiquities," Reynes said, still watching. "And a classical guitar stood upright on a stand in the corner. At first, the director claimed none of his scientists were missing. However, when called in for confirmation, his assistant said Dr. Thompson missed a meeting that morning with Professor Norbert Willington."

"How did he react to the news of Thompson's death?" I asked.

"A little shocked but not like he'd lost a dear friend," Reynes said.

"What's our next step?"

Reynes started to move toward the door. "Thompson worked with two other scientists here, Dr. Alexander Burroughs, a renowned Lepidopterist, and Dr. Antoine Denis, a French botanist. Their offices are in the basement, our next stop."

As he reached the door, Reynes turned to the secretary and asked, "Miss, can you tell me where to find Professor Willington?"

"At his office over at Oxford," she snapped. "Where else?"

When we reached the corridor, I had to ask.

"What were you looking at behind me?"

"The Russian secretary," he said. "When she thought we weren't looking, she secreted some papers inside her blouse."

"What do you think she took?"

"No way to know until we learn more," Reynes said.

"Did you tell the director about the leaf?"

"I showed him the leaf," Reynes said. "He identified it as coming from a Baobab tree, genus Adansonia digitata - found only in middle Africa."

"Is that significant?"

"I don't know," Reynes said, leading the way down a stairway to the basement.

We exited the stairwell into the basement corridor, continued down the hall to a door that read, "Entomology," and entered. The large room was open with three desks spaced equidistant amidst vast amounts of clutter – chests with drawers for specimens, laboratory benches covered with equipment, books spilling out of their bookcases onto the floor.

On the first desk, a name plate read Dr. Alexander Burroughs. Behind the desk sat a big soft man with gentle brown eyes. Across the room, I could see the desk of Dr. Antoine Denis. Denis, a short, skinny man with a narrow face and long Parisian nose stooped over his desk working in rubber gloves on something apparently caustic. The remaining desk had to be Thompson's. As I approached Burroughs, Reynes went directly to the murdered man's desk, sat down, and began looking through his papers.

"Hello," I said. "I am Colonel Forster, and my associate is Mr. Carvel Reynes. We would like to ask you about Dr. Thompson."

"The director's assistant called ahead to tell us what happened, and that you were coming down," Burroughs said.

Neither of them showed emotion.

"Ask your questions to us simultaneously," Denis said. "We're busy."

"Tell us about Dr. Thompson," I said.

"I didn't know him well," Burroughs said. "I started here the month before he left for Africa."

"I didn't know him at all," Denis said. "I started here ten weeks after he arrived in Africa."

Reynes abruptly rose and circled the room. "Are these Thompson's?" he asked, pointing to the crates stacked along the wall near Thompson's desk.

"Yes," Burroughs said.

Reynes walked to the first stack of crates. The top one was open, and he dug into it, pulling out leaves matching the one found in Thompson's pocket. In another crate, he found a notebook and a corked test tube half-filled with a black tar-like substance, sealed with wax. He sat down at Thompson's desk and began reading notebook entries. Moving to look over his shoulder, I saw a drawing of the same leaf, labeled Erthrophleum suaveolens. Below the drawings was a recipe titled Ngwele - calling for the bark and seeds of the aforementioned plant plus three others: Strychnos icaja (stems),

51

Palisota borteri (leaves), and Combretum (stems). Below this recipe was written: "Compare symptoms with Parke."

"Did Thompson share his discoveries with either of you?" Reynes asked.

"Only mentioning that his findings would be of great interest to the museum director," Burroughs said. "In my opinion, his discoveries, if substantial, would have increased his standing among the scientific community. Africa is the popular frontier now."

"He said nothing to me," Denis said.

Reynes signaled me to follow him. Apparently, our investigation here was finished. As we reached the corridor and closed the door, he whispered, "Colonel, in the morning, we shall interview Professor Willington. I will send word ahead."

We found Professor Willington in his office on the third floor of the Great Hall of University College at Oxford, standing by the window reading a book. He was a kindly-looking older man with wisps of grey hair, a slight stoop, wearing rumbled clothes.

"Professor, our apologies for disturbing you," Reynes said.

"Non-student visitors are always a welcome change," the professor said. "How may I assist?"

"We're investigating Dr. Leonard Thompson's death" Reynes said.

"Oh, dear," the professor said. "We've lost a brilliant scientist   one of my past students who occasionally came to me for research advice."

"What did he want to discuss yesterday?" Reynes asked.

The professor stared for a moment, sizing us up. "What are your military backgrounds?" he asked.

"I served in the Light Brigade in the Crimean War and 20 years with Scotland Yard," I said.

"I served in Army Intelligence for four years and as a private detective for ten," Reynes said.

"Good. I must rely on your honor as officers not to disclose what I tell you," the professor said.

We both agreed.

"Thompson was serving in Her Majesty's Secret Service under the cover of his exploration," the professor said. "He was reporting to me on the French colonization."

"Why did he want to meet?" Reynes asked.

"He sent a message that his life was in danger, and he had important information for me," the professor said. "I sent word for him to come at once. He included a cipher with his message that I have been unable to decode."

He handed Reynes a piece of paper on which the following three lines were handwritten:

Baobab

DE   PY

364414

"Perhaps I can decipher this," Reynes said.

"Let me know if you do," the professor said.

We descended the worn stairs to the ground level. As we exited, we passed a monument that stopped Reynes in his tracks - a statue of Surgeon-General Thomas Haezle Parke honoring his African discoveries.

"This must be the Parke that Thompson mentioned in his notes," Reynes said. "We need to know more about this man."

We returned to Reynes' apartment. As we entered, Reynes stooped to retrieve an envelope that had been slipped under his door. He opened it and quickly read the message.

"Colonel, the coroner reports the cause of death as an unknown poison," he said. "Thompson's lungs were filled with black blood." After staring out the window for a moment, he said, "There are multiple forces at work in this matter, but I can't sort them out."

"Maybe the cipher will help," I said.

Reynes pulled out the paper with the cipher on it, laid it on his dining table and brushed it flat. He sat down and pulled over a chair, motioning for me to sit next to him. He and I worked on the cipher for several hours, applying various substitutions and transpositions, but without success.

"It is time to let it rest for the night," Reynes finally said. "We'll continue fresh in the morning."

I departed and returned to my flat for sustenance and rest.

When I arrived back at Reynes' apartment the next morning, Reynes was dressed in yesterday's clothes. Apparently, he hadn't slept and was still deep in concentration. As I entered, he was fanning through a botany book. He motioned for me to sit quietly while he finished.

"Ah hah!" he said.

I sat quietly and watched as Reynes jotted a note. He looked back and forth between the book, the cipher, and his notepaper, and he began crossing out letters from what he had written. Suddenly, he leapt to his feet, pulled me up, and pushed me toward the door, grabbing his coat and hat on the way.

"Colonel, get an inspector and a half-dozen bobbys and bring them to the museum director's office. I will round up the suspects. By the time we've gathered, I hope to have worked out what happened."

We both dashed off.

When I arrived at the director's office with an inspector and the bobbys, Reynes had assembled the director, the two basement scientists, the professor, and the director's assistant. Entering the director's office was like entering a microcosm of the entire museum with artifacts decorating every shelf and wall. The director sat behind his large desk. The two scientists seemed to repel each other like opposing poles of a pair of magnets. The professor sat in one office wing chair and Tatiana, the assistant, sat in the other, but on the edge of her seat. Reynes was pacing back and forth, still thinking.

"When did you last see Dr. Thompson?" Reynes asked Tatiana, who played nervously with her long blond locks.

"Late on the afternoon of the night he died, when he arrived to meet with the director," she said. "I then left for home."

"The cipher that Thompson sent to Professor Willington identified a spy working here at the museum," Reynes said, looking directly at Tatiana. She bolted for the door. A policeman grabbed her arm as she passed.

"Arrest her," Reynes said. "You will find she has been spying for the Russians."

"How did you know?" she asked.

"I didn't," Reynes said. "You weren't the spy Thompson revealed to us. I just suspected from seeing you steal documents while we stood talking in your lobby."

"Then, who's the spy Thompson identified?" the Yard inspector asked.

"Solving the cipher required the use of the scientific name of the baobab tree, Adansonia digitata. He wrote the common name above the codes as a clue but would naturally, as a scientist, have used the Latin name. Extracting the unduplicated letters in the Latin name provides the letters ADNSOIDGT," Reynes said. "Using the numbers from the cipher, 3646414, to select letters from this list and inserting those letters between letters on the second line of the cipher, between the DE and the PY, yields the sentence, 'Denis is a spy'."

"Denis?" Owens asked.

"Denis has been spying for the French," Reynes said. "When Thompson arrived in Africa, the French became suspicious and dispatched their spy to the museum to confirm their suspicions. The Colonel will recall that Denis knew the exact number of weeks, as he said, 'after Thompson's arrival in Africa' not 'after his departure for Africa.' Denis was in Africa when Thompson arrived and when the spy was sent to London. Customs can confirm his origin and the date he arrived. As a museum employee, Denis also could mingle with other scientists and steal their discoveries for France's military."

Two policemen restrained the red-faced Denis.

"Which spy killed Dr. Thompson?" the inspector asked.

"A reasonable question," Reynes said. "Especially since the victim had written on the floor with his saliva what looked like the letter D and one spy is named Denis, and the other is named Demidova. However, neither is our murderer."

"Then, who is?" I asked.

"Let me explain," Reynes said. "The first key to this mystery required three clues: The leaves from Thompson's pocket, the notebook and vial found among his discoveries, and former Surgeon-General Parke. From last night's research, I learned Dr. Parke was the first explorer to discover the African Pigmy tribe and the poison arrows they used to kill enemies and prey. He discovered the poison but not the formula. According to the notebook, Thompson discovered the formula for making the poison - important to science and the military. The leaves, recipe, and sample he brought back for further study prove his discovery. His discovery got him killed, and his discovery is what killed him."

"So, who poisoned him?" I asked. "That poison vial you found was sealed."

"The second key was Thompson himself," Reynes said. "He realized he had been poisoned and hurried to see Holmes with the hope he might save him or at least exact justice on his killer, not knowing, because he had been out of the country that Holmes had disappeared. From his notes, Thompson knew the poison was water-soluble and slow-acting - a small dose taking eight to twelve hours to kill a human adult. When he realized he had been poisoned, he went to Holmes, thinking his dose had been small, and he had some time. He died as he arrived at Holmes' apartment because he received a larger dose than he had thought."

"But where would a large dose of the poison come from?" I asked. "Were there other vials?"

"Not according to Thompson's notes," Reynes said. "A search of the museum display honoring Parke will find pigmy arrows that have a mixture of poison and tea on their tips. Tea on the arrows will prove they were used to stir tea - the tea Thompson drank on the evening he came to see the director."

"That doesn't clarify who the killer is," the inspector said.

"Professional jealousy was the killer," Reynes said. "As Thompson went into the muscular rigor that he recognized as the final stage of the poison, he used his saliva to try to write the name of his killer on the floor but was only able to scribble one letter. I thought the letter was a D, but it was a malformed O, with the last portion of his scribble pulled straight by his arm's final contraction."

"Are you saying Director Owens is Thompson's killer?" the inspector asked.

"Yes," Reynes said. "He stood to lose the most from Thompson's discovery. Owens idolized Surgeon-General Parke. Owen erected the statue to Parke at Oxford. And with Thompson having advanced Parkes's discoveries to new heights, Thompson would have eclipsed Owen in the scientific community. Thompson might even have become the leading candidate for the presidency of the Royal Society, which Owens could not bear or chance. Owens was the one who opened Thompson's crate. He saw in the notebook the significance of Thompson's discoveries. He knew the crates contained other discoveries that he could claim as his own - to enhance his career with Thompson out of the way."

"You can't prove this," Owens said.

"I have two other deductions that will," Reynes said. "First, you told me the leaves from Thompson's pocket were from a baobab tree. You're an expert in this field. However, my research found the leaves came from a tree called Erythrophleum suaveolens – the plant from which the poison is made. You intentionally misidentified the leaves to mislead us. Second, we have this." Reynes pulled his handkerchief from his pocket and showed the fingernail. "I saw the classical guitar in your office. Serious guitarists develop calluses on the fingers of their left hand and grow long nails on the fingers of their right."

The inspector grabbed Owens' hands. "Sure enough," he said. "Calluses on his left hand."

"But look at the nails on my right hand —neat and even," Owens said, holding his hand up for everyone to see.

"Yes, trimmed back to the length of the broken nail - trimmed even, so when grown out, they can again serve as guitar picks," Reynes said. "Inspector, under a microscope you should be able to match the lateral striations in this nail with one of the nails on his right hand."

"Thompson must have found the nail by the opened crate and realized who had opened it," I said. "That is why he went to the director – to confront him about his snooping."

"Yes. Knowing Thompson asked for an appointment to see him, the director prepared the tea," Reynes said.

"Bastard!" Owens yelled. "You've ruined me."

Owens grabbed a dagger from a wall display and charged at Reynes, but before he closed the distance, policemen grabbed and held him.

"Dr. Owens, you're under arrest for Dr. Thompson's murder," the inspector said.

On the way home, we stopped to give Mrs. Hudson the news.

"Mr. Holmes would have been proud of you, Mr. Reynes," she said.

"Oh, it was nothing," he said.

"Holmes' books and treatises remain in his apartment. Perhaps you might consider moving in upstairs."

"I would not presuppose to fill Holmes' shoes, let alone his apartment,' Reynes said. "Who knows? Perhaps he is still alive and will return one day."

Vellore India -- 1856

Being blindfolded, Sgt. Major Malloy's eyes could not tell him to what part of the city he had been dragged, bound, and gagged. Based on the time that passed and initial direction taken since being yanked rudely from a peaceful park bench in the city square, he reckoned he had been hauled to the northern outskirts of the city, towards Katpadi. Knowing his location gave him little comfort because he had no reason to hope for rescue, even though hundreds of his fellow British troops were garrisoned in the city.

When his kidnappers removed his blindfold, and his eyes adjusted to the dark of the night, he could see the outline of an old building with a low, slanting roof. He could see its tan walls of baked mud. As his captors pushed him inside, he recognized a smell , the building had been used for leather tanning, a common business in Vellore. He also had an emerging and distasteful idea of why his captors had brought to this place. The five men who forced him to this dilapidated building had to be Hindu Sepoys out of uniform and hell-bent on revenge. His death, for simply being a British soldier, would likely only be the first of many others . The Sepoys had been badly abused by the British military for over 20 years, and every British soldier in the city sensed they were on the verge of rising up.

Once inside the building, they dragged Malloy across the dusty floor and stood him up on the brink of a gaping hole, a pit about six feet across, with a depth indiscernible because of the darkness. Two Sepoys passed a rope, wrapped with a soft cloth, around his waist. His hands were already tied similarly behind his back. The purpose of padding the evil ropes, he deduced, was to avoid leaving telltale marks on his body.

With the end of the rope tossed over a beam and pulled taut, and a pull from the same strong arms that had roughly handled him to this place, they lifted and swung his body up and over the gaping mouth of the pit and began lowering him into the darkness. Just as his eyes passed below ground level, he thought he caught a glimpse of his army mate, Sgt. Major Rodney McDougal, chief engineer for the 18th (The Royal Irish), at a small window. McDougal must have seen Malloy's captors jump him and followed. If anyone could save Malloy, McDougal would be the one who could do it. However, the odds of five strong Sepoys against one British soldier were stacked too heavily, even for a robust man like McDougal. Besides, neither of them could tell in the surrounding darkness whether any of the five men were armed. He suspected McDougal would wait for the right opening but doubted he would be in time. In his heart, he knew he had only seconds left in his life.

They lowered him slowly and painfully. About fifteen feet down into the abyss, his feet touched – soil, thank God. His relief in feeling solid dry ground, as he had expected water to be his grave, was fleeting. He began to feel the sides of the pit, but they offered him no hope – no foot or handholds, no ladder, no way up or out. His mind immediately snapped to what to expect next. Would they leave him here to die of dehydration and starvation? Would they shovel dirt over him and bury him alive? What was their plan? He considered what McDougal must be thinking. His friend had no way to see what was happening yet must realize the extreme urgency and dire outlook of the impending danger. It was clear to Malloy that the intentions of the Sepoys were hostile and meant to culminate in some painful way in his death. As his mind sifted through the possibilities, he concluded being smothered under dirt would be the form of death he dreaded the most.

India can be dangerous at any time of the day, as treachery abounds for British soldiers posted to the far reaches of this mysterious country. McDougal and Malloy had just begun seven-day liberty and were out on the town searching for diversion when this began. McDougal had wandered off in search of a dram of whiskey while Malloy chose to wait in the city's main plaza and watch local citizens going about their daily routines. Malloy's predicament started about thirty minutes after arriving, not long after sitting down on a park bench with an open view of the square. As he sat quietly near the town plaza, a young woman, with raven-black hair and eyes to match, sat down and sidled up next to him. His initial reaction was flattery that she would sit next to him, but his second reaction was suspicion. This was not London, and her behavior was inappropriate for this part of the world. He should have recognized the threat because Indian women did not show attention in public, let alone affection.

Suddenly, she began tearing her clothes and then attacked and scratched his face. Next, she began screaming that Malloy had attacked her and in seconds five men appeared, claiming to be witnesses to the attack. The men quickly blindfolded him, bound his hands and upper arms, and dragged him away. Sullying a woman in India was a capital offense. In a British court, Malloy might have hope of defending himself; however, in Vellore, India, he understood instantly that a formal court of law would not pronounce his sentence.

Initially, He resisted as best he could, as a Sgt. Major would, but his captors overpowered him. He soon exhausted himself, sporadically renewing his struggle from time to time as they pushed, pulled, and dragged him to this place. His repeated resistance fatigued him thoroughly.

He assumed these Sepoys had staged this fake crime and taken the law into their hands because they had been mistreated. These men sought revenge for their fellow soldiers, killed when British troops put down Sepoy rebellions in Meerut, Lucknow, and Cawnpore a year ago. Vellore had a similar rebellion put down in 1806. The remaining survivors of that earlier uprising had not forgotten the humiliation and the executions of their friends and family. The city's Sepoys had carried ill will toward British soldiers for over fifty years, a long-held anger, rekindled by the British actions of the previous year. Their smoldering anger inflamed the rage of today's younger Sepoys, fanned by their natural strong sympathy with their brothers in arms in the recent conflict to the north.

The revolution in the north began when an oblivious military engineer back in London produced and distributed to the field bullets with coated paper wrappers, the ends of which the Sepoys would have to bite off. The engineer had ordered the bullets coated, for water-proofing, with the lard of pigs and cows. Touching pigs and cows deeply offended both the Hindus and the Muslims. This offense meant thousands of Sepoys stationed with British troops across India became convinced that the East India Company and British monarchy were contriving to force them into becoming Christians, which they greatly resented. Malloy remembered that irresponsible act of one man, far away in London over a year ago, and knew the cause of his impending death.

Being July, with day temperatures well above one hundred degrees and night temperatures still over ninety, Malloy perspired profusely from the exertion as well as his fear, the only good omen at that moment. Once his body ceased perspiring, it would mean dehydration was on its way to kill him.

He could hear the Sepoys talking, but not being fully conversant with their language, especially their idioms and slang, he could understand only snatches of what they said. Suddenly, he felt the rope slacken and land at its full length at his feet. Any glimmer of hope for an escape, if one could still be imagined, was now fully extinguished. Even so, he remained calm, an eerie calm that came over him like a gazelle held in a lion's mouth. He remained in this suspended state until he heard the words, "*Naja Naja.*" His whole body jumped without leaving the ground, and his skin crawled at the sound of the name – the name for the Indian Cobra, smaller cousin to the King Cobra, but just as deadly.

Snakes terrify most humans and Malloy stood tall among those most terrified. While some people may think the creatures are slimy, those who have touched them know they are scaly and dry. However, he did not fear the touch of their skin; he feared the pain that follows their bite. As an instinct, human fear of snakes must have begun when our early ancestors first discovered the slow and painful death that followed snakebite. Even with his years of army experience in India, Malloy could not identify every poisonous snake, but he could recognize an Indian cobra when he saw one. A single bite would kill a victim in three out of four occurrences. Cobras can bite repeatedly, and multiple bites from a cobra result in an agonizing death. The notion of encountering a snake is by itself fearful – its silent approach, the sudden unexpected pain of dual punctures, and the immediate realization that hope is lost. Malloy knew the reality was far worse. The whole process of dying from a snake bite can take an excruciatingly painful hour. The thought made him vomit.

The gist of the conversation he heard was that the Sepoys were about to drop a cobra into the pit to serve as his executioner, so his death would appear to be an accident. Of course, if McDougal broke into the building to attempt his rescue, after the cobra had been dropped into the pit, and if the snake had not yet bitten him, the sudden noise could cause it to do so.

Then, to Malloy's shock, not one but dozens of cobras began to rain down on him. They were hitting his head, falling at his feet, and swarming around him. He could just barely see as his eyes had adjusted partially to the darkness. He could see two cobras attacking each other. He knew his legs would be next. Despair for his survival filled his mind and heart. He struggled to hold every muscle still while knowing the time of his remaining life had run down to seconds. Cobras can feel vibrations, sense heat, and see up to three hundred feet. He believed they sensed fear too.

Then, Malloy heard the Sepoys move off and heard a door slam shut and lock. He could feel death crawling around his feet. Even if McDougal could break in now, he had no way to save Malloy from the snakes or even to pull him out of this pit. Malloy would not dare reach for the loose end of the rope or to attempt to throw it up to McDougal.

Then he heard a dripping noise. The sound of drips slowly turned into the sound of water trickling , running down one side of the pit. The added fear of drowning compounded his inner panic. Gradually, the flow of water increased until it ran in a steady stream down all sides of the pit, steadily filling the pit with water.

The snakes started moving in a wide circle – swarming around the edges of the pit on the surface of the water as the pit began to fill. With no drain, the flow, if sufficient, would eventually fill the pit. However, with his hands tied behind his back, the water would likely drown him in the process - if the snakes did not bite him first. McDougal had found a way to divert a water flow into this building and into the pit – an unexpected and amazing engineering feat, but one Malloy feared would fail.

Malloy knew how to swim, but he also knew that thrashing his arms around and kicking his legs under water could excite the snakes into biting. So, he went into a dead man's float, an appropriate name in the circumstance where he kept his body as vertically as he could while bending his head as far back as possible, holding his breath and letting his body and head sink to where only his mouth protruded above water. He could feel snakes brushing and occasionally swimming right over his face. He could not help but swallow and gag on the water. He forced himself to control his gags when snakes were crossing his face, so he would not startle them.

Finally, the pit filled with water. As it reached the top, the snakes begin to crawl out and slither away into the various crannies of the building. Before long, they were gone and McDougal arrived to grab him by his arms and hoist Malloy's exhausted, unscathed body, out of the pit, alive.

Within days, Malloy and his mates tracked down and arrested the perpetrators. When asked what became of them, he would only mutter, "Their punishment involved snakes." He never elaborated.

Yet the experience left more than bruises and nightmares. From that day on, whenever Malloy walked alone, he listened for the faint drip in the silence, for the scratch of scales across the ground. He would sometimes smile at danger, not from bravado, but from deeper knowledge. He had looked death in the eye and walked away. The pit had tried him, but it had not claimed him. And in that narrow space between terror and survival, something within him had shifted. He no longer feared the dark.

And in India, that alone set him apart.

Albany -- NY

On a crisp October evening, just as the clock struck nine, Ginny, the blonde clerk for the Albany Police Department's detective squad, strode into Lieutenant Jack Franzen's office. The faint hum of the city filtered through the window, a reminder of the world beyond the precinct walls.

"Lieutenant Franzen, patrol's bringing in three burglary suspects," Ginny announced, her voice cutting through the stillness. "Can you stay to interview them?"

Franzen sighed, glancing at the stack of paperwork on his desk. "With everyone else gone, I'm the last line of defense. So much for wrapping up the Mahoney case tonight." He rose, filed the documents away, and turned as two patrolmen ushered in a peculiar trio.

The first suspect hobbled in on arm crutches, his hunched frame marking him as an invalid. Behind him trailed a tall, gaunt woman draped in a flowing black gown and shawl, her haggard features stark against the dim light. The third was a young man, barely five feet tall, his rotund figure straining every seam of his clothes as if one wrong move might split them apart. They were a motley crew, unlike any burglars Franzen had ever encountered.

"What have we got here?" Franzen asked, eyebrow raised.

"Caught these two lurking by the St. Francis convent on 16th and Howard," one patrolman said, gesturing to the invalid and the woman. "She had a bag with a drill, screwdriver, hammer, and, strangely, a toaster."

The second patrolman nodded toward the heavyset youth. "Found this one in a car around the corner. Admitted he was waiting for them."

"Take them to interview room one," Franzen instructed. "I'll be there shortly."

"We've only got one interview room," the first patrolman replied.

Franzen smirked. "I know. They don't."

Grabbing his coffee, anticipating a long night, Franzen entered the interview room and settled across from the trio. The patrolmen stood sentinel behind them. Up close, the suspects were even more striking. The invalid, middle-aged with a mop of black hair and bushy brows sat with a slight tilt, his crutches propped beside him. The woman, likely in her fifties, had stringy dark hair and a mole sprouting wiry strands on her pointed chin, a caricature of a witch. The young man's girth obscured his belt entirely, his round face glistening with nervous sweat.

"So, who's the mastermind?" Franzen asked, his tone dry. The patrolmen stifled grins.

"I'm our spokesperson," the invalid said, his voice steady. "Rodney Jarrett. I own the bookstore on 17th, off Wheeler."

"What were you doing at the convent at nine at night?" Franzen pressed.

"Delivering the tools and toaster the officers confiscated," Rodney replied.

Franzen leaned forward. "You were caught after dark, skulking around a convent in a rough neighborhood. It's dangerous even in daylight."

"We know," Rodney said. "We live there."

"Was the convent expecting your... delivery?" Franzen asked.

"No," Rodney admitted.

"So, you brought tools and a toaster to a closed convent, uninvited, in the dead of night. That right?"

"Pretty much," Rodney said.

"Why?" Franzen asked, incredulity creeping into his voice.

"I couldn't say," Rodney replied.

"Can't or won't?" Franzen challenged.

"Both," Rodney said with a faint shrug.

"Playing clever, huh?" Franzen said. "If you don't explain, I'll have to lock you up for suspected burglary."

"We weren't stealing," Rodney countered. "We were delivering."

"That's what they all say," Franzen shot back. "Without a reason, you're staying in custody."

"Then do what you must," Rodney said calmly.

The trio rose as one, Rodney lifting his crutches, the others extending their hands for cuffs. Franzen waved the patrolmen off. "No cuffs. Take them away. Tomorrow, check the convent, see if those items were stolen."

The next morning, a patrolman returned with news. "Mother Superior didn't know the suspects. The convent doesn't own those tools or a toaster. But she said they'd be useful, their soup kitchen's being renovated."

Franzen rubbed his chin. "Good Samaritans, maybe? But why the secrecy?"

"Maybe they'll talk to the judge this afternoon," the patrolman suggested.

The three stood before the judge in court, flanked by a public defender. "Charged with attempted burglary, Your Honor," the prosecutor declared.

"How do you plead?" the judge asked.

"Not guilty," they chorused.

"Evidence?" the judge prompted.

"Caught with burglary tools, and a toaster, on the convent steps at 9 p.m.," the prosecutor said.

"A toaster?" the judge echoed, bemused.

"Yes, Your Honor," Rodney interjected.

"You admit you were there with these items?" the judge asked.

"Yes," Rodney replied.

"What were you doing?" the judge inquired.

"They won't say, Your Honor," their attorney answered.

"Won't say?" the judge pressed. "Not even to you?"

"That's right," the attorney confirmed.

"Are they invoking the Fifth?"

"Not that I know," the attorney said.

The judge stared at the trio, baffled. "Did the convent report these items as stolen?"

"No, Your Honor," the prosecutor admitted. "But they could use them for their soup kitchen."

"Hold on," the judge said. "You're charging them with attempted burglary, but nothing was taken?"

"It's about intent," the prosecutor argued. "The tools suggest they planned to break in."

"With a toaster?" the judge asked, incredulously.

"Could've been from a prior theft," the prosecutor ventured.

"I'm not convinced," the judge said. "What valuables does a convent even have?"

Rodney slipped a paper from his pocket and offered it forward. The attorney passed it to the judge via the bailiff.

"A receipt for the toaster," the attorney explained.

The judge examined it. "This undermines your case." He turned to Rodney. "Receipts for the tools?"

"No, Your Honor," Rodney said. "They're from my bookstore toolbox, my father bought them years ago."

The judge eyed the pristine tools. "They look unused."

Rodney raised his crutches with a shrug, hinting at his limited mobility.

"So," the judge mused, "you were delivering a purchased toaster and unused tools to a convent that didn't request them but could use them?"

The woman and youth nodded eagerly.

"Why?" the judge asked.

"We can't say," Rodney replied.

Spectators tittered. The judge studied them, then ventured, "Were you leaving them as a donation, knowing their need?"

Rodney nodded.

"Why not just say so?" the judge asked.

Rodney gestured toward the chamber's door.

"In private?" the judge clarified. "Fifteen-minute recess. Bring them to my chambers."

In chambers, the judge demanded, "Why all the mystery?"

"We swore not to tell," the woman, Abigail, said.

"It started two months ago," Rodney began. "My bookstore barely sustains me. My father set it up before he

73

died, given my cerebral palsy. It is a meager living, supplemented by aid, but I am an outcast, mocked, stared at, shunned. Abigail was browsing my shelves one day, hiding from her own tormentors. Then Willy burst in, fleeing bullies targeting his weight. We bonded over our shared isolation."

"And the tools?" the prosecutor snapped.

"We discussed revenge," Rodney continued, "but decided to channel our intellect into secret good deeds instead. The convent's kitchen renovation was our latest act. We work at night to avoid judgment; people assume the worst of us."

"You've done this before?" the judge asked.

"Yes," Rodney said. "Food drops, fence repairs, alley cleanups, small acts with what little we have. We vowed anonymity to preserve our dignity, not for gain."

"We're delivering textbooks to the school next week," Willy added.

The judge nodded slowly. "You're harmless," he said at last. "Case dismissed, records expunged. Any objections, prosecutor?"

"None, Your Honor."

"Gag order on both attorneys," the judge continued. "No leaks, or it's contempt."

He stood, gathering his papers. As they all began to file out, the judge leaned toward Rodney and asked, almost casually, "So—what day and time do you usually plan your next move?"

DRIVING THROUGH WESTERN VIRGINIA

Returning from a demanding overnight business trip through the mountains of West Virginia, Brian, a business associate, and I stopped for lunch at Kathy's Diner in the small town of Staunton, just across the state line from West Virginia, in Virginia. Staunton is "nestled in the foothills of the Shenandoah Mountains," as the town describes itself. I would describe it as a small town at a crossroad in the middle of rolling wooded hills. Kathy's Diner had the look of a place where we could find southern home cooking and perhaps a glimpse into the southern frame of mind. Delightfully, we found both or at least I did.

Staunton is a small town like so many others dotting the eastern slope of the Appalachian mountain range and well-represents the local charm of this part of the world. Its main distinction is having been Woodrow Wilson's birthplace. Seeing it for my first and only time made me think that possibly not much had happened there since.

We were on our way home from two days of complicated business negotiations at a remote ski resort five hours back west, in West Virginia. On our way home to the urban environs of Norfolk, Virginia, Brian and I couldn't help but reflect on the contrast of our big-city lives with those of Staunton's residents.

Upon entering the diner, I fully expected that we would be seated by the proprietor, Kathy, herself; however, according to the photos on the wall, the proprietor either wasn't the pleasant silver-haired lady seating us or the photos had been taken a long time ago. She led us to a booth with bench seats covered in red plastic located along the windows. I sat on the side facing the door, where we had entered.

Behind me in the next booth sat two elderly ladies facing each other, as Brian would tell me later, since I never turned around to see them. One was talking very loudly, possibly because she was hard of hearing, or because her friend was, or maybe because she just didn't know her volume, and her friend was polite in not telling her. She had to be the one facing in the same direction as I was, toward the door - facing the back of my head, because I could hear her very clearly, better than Brian could, sitting across from me. He later claimed he didn't hear what I heard.

Brian abandoned our mission of seeking home cooking and ordered a turkey sandwich. I remained true to the plan and ordered the daily special, homemade fried chicken, mashed potatoes with gravy and collard greens. We discussed our recent business meeting while we waited for our food. Our food arrived at the slower pace one expects in the south; however, when it came it lived up to expectations in both appearance and taste.

As we ate, the loud-talking lady started a conversation that made me stop talking and smile with the simplicity of her statements, delivered in her rich Virginia southern drawl.

"I turned on the TV," she said, pausing for a long time. "I tried watching it for a while. Then I turned it off."

She spoke slowly and deliberately, almost as if reluctant to get to the point. I couldn't help thinking to myself, "So, you turned on the TV and ... then what?"

After a pause, she continued, "I then got up and went to look for a book to read. However, I couldn't find one that interested me."

To myself, I thought, "okay, and then what?" I continued to listen - fascinated by her melodic voice and the southern pace of the conversation.

Then she said, "After a while I came back and turned on the TV again." She paused, "I started to watch a mystery; however, I couldn't tell you anything about it."

This conversation about seemingly nothing moved at a snail's pace, gave no clue as to where it might go next, yet had me hanging on every word.

Then she said, "So I turned off the TV again, but just as it was going off, I heard something about an eclipse of the moon. I thought I would let the dog out and take a look."

As I listened to the lady talk, I began to wonder why her words were so captivating. Why was this simple conversation between two elderly ladies in this cozy little diner in a quiet little town holding my attention? I wasn't sure. Perhaps it was some vague titillation from eavesdropping on a life so different from mine?

She continued, "The dog did her thing, a couple of times I think, and I looked up and could see the full moon but no eclipse. It must have been going on somewhere else, or maybe I was too early or too late or just didn't hear the announcer correctly."

Her friend kept making understanding noises, like "Uh-huh, Uh-huh."

The lady continued, "After a while, I came in and, since it was about 2:30 in the morning, I thought I should go to bed, but that's when I normally get up to get ready to go to work so I wasn't sure I could sleep."

It seemed her life had taken some kind of turn.

Her friend mentioned something about, she could never get up for work at 2:30AM and didn't know how this lady could have done so for so many years. No mention was made as to what kind of work the lady did to make her living or why she hadn't been able to go to sleep earlier.

The lady continued, "I went to bed but just thrashed around for hours. The bed got to where it looked like fifteen people had slept it in. I hadn't slept at all."

That made me laugh to myself. I knew about that. I've often thrashed, tossing and turning all night, getting no sleep.

She continued, "After a while longer, I got up and remade the bed. I then lay back down to try to sleep, and finally, did fall asleep. I slept for some time but dreamed heavily. I dreamt through the whole thing all over again."

"I dreamt through the whole thing all over again?" I asked myself. "What did that mean? What had she lived through?"

Then she said, "I awoke, and I am sure I was awake, and George was there. We talked. He told me everything would be okay. That I was alone now and had to take care of myself. He said that we would be together again later and everything would be fine. Then he was gone; for now, until later."

I stopped listening at this point as her remarks overloaded my brain. I couldn't reconcile what I had heard with my own reality. My mind kept going back over what she had just said.

We finished our meal and prepared to leave. As I walked to the cashier stand near the door to pay my check, I didn't look back. I didn't want to spoil the image of this beautiful elderly lady whom I had created in my mind; I wanted to hold onto this intimate moment in a small Appalachian town; and I wanted to remember what it means to live a simple life and to love someone so deeply and then to lose them – but, then to recognize that everything will be okay and being alone will only be for a time.

Georgia -- 1950

Billy Mathias labored five days a week on a chain gang in the heart of the South Georgia swamps, where the weather was often hot and often rainy. Billy was too old for the rigor of chain gang work, but the Bulls still made him do it. He was sixty-five years old, grey-haired, sparsely, and walked with a limp from a childhood accident and a family that couldn't afford medical treatment.

Billy worked on what was called the "rail gang," had done so for twenty-five years and was the oldest member of that gang. Carl Wilson, though five years younger than Billy, was the gang's trustee because he had been in prison a year longer than Billy.

The rail gang reworked railroad tracks. They pulled up old spikes, replaced deteriorated ties, sometimes laid-in new rails and always pounded in new spikes to hold the tracks from shifting as trains rolled over. They helped the trains travel to places Billy could only dream of going – taking people to see sights he would never see. He was in prison for life. He was resigned to his fate; except for two wishes -- two impossible dreams – that he hoped could somehow happen before his end came. It is not unusual for a man in a hopeless situation to still have hopes and dreams. They helped Billy face his endless days.

On a typical day, the chain gang would be shackled together right after breakfast, at 7:30AM sharp; and then trucked and marched to a remote section of track, on which the crew would work. The gang returned to the prison around

6:00 PM each evening. The work was backbreaking, especially for a man of Billy's age. The Boss Man, a pot-bellied redneck Bull, supervised the ever-changing set of guards who watched over the gang daily. The Boss Man had ruled over the chain gang for twenty years – nearly as long as Billy had served on it. He hated Billy on his first day and still did. The Boss Man wouldn't think of excusing Billy from hard labor even one day earlier than the law directed - at age seventy. Billy expected that the work would kill him before he reached seventy.

On a late summer day, the twelve prisoners were hammering spikes in rhythm to an old Negro spiritual. The rhythm aided their breathing, kept their minds off the toil and made their day go by faster. They had been pulling and hammering for half a day when Carl, the trustee, walked over from the guard truck and told them to stop for lunch, a simple meal consisting of stale bread and old cheese. After twenty minutes, the Boss Man ordered them back to work.

When the Boss Man and the two guards weren't looking and out of ear shot, the prisoners would quietly talk.

"How long ya been doin' this?" a white prisoner named Jason asked.

"Twenty-five and forever to go," Billy said.

"I'm in my first year of ten, and it feel like forever already," Jason said. "How'd ya do it?"

Billy answered, "One spike at a time."

"Well, I'll be looking for an opening to run," Jason said.

"Don't try it," Billy said. "They got sharp aim with 'em guns and if you get past 'em, they got dogs, smart dogs with powerful noses. Dem dogs don't quit. Nobody's made it yet. I knew men that didn't get brought back after I've heard they were caught -- alive."

"I won't be able to stay caged up like this for much longer," Jason said.

"You'll get used to it," Billy said. "Give yourself another year or two and you'll settle into a routine."

At the other end of the work line, a prisoner asked the Boss Man for water.

"No!" the Boss Man shouted. "Not enough work's been done since your break. Get back to work."

The prisoners and the guards dripped with sweat from the beating sun. The prisoner looked menacingly at the man. The Boss Man motioned to the closest guard, who knew from the motion that he was to train his shotgun on the prisoner.

"Is this prisoner escaping his chains?" the Boss Man asked the guard with a sneer.

Successfully intimidated, the prisoner slinked back to hammering and the guard shouldered his gun again.

Back on the other end of the work line, Jason asked Billy, "Why are you here for life?"

"Killed a man," Billy said, as he drove in a spike three-quarters of the way with a single blow of his sledgehammer.

"He musta had it comin', right?" Jason asked.

"No, he didn't," Billy said. "They gave me what I deserved."

"You ever think of running?" Jason asked.

"Used to dream about runnin'," Billy said. "But I know why da law put me here and da law was right. So here I'll remain 'til I die."

"So, that's it?" Jason asked. "No regrets, nothing left for you?"

"There's two things I still'd like to do," he said. "But ain't expectin' to do 'em 'til after I die."

"What would they be?" Jason asked.

The boss man saw them talking. "Three days in the box if you talk again, Billy" he said.

#

A month later, Billy and his cell mate Tom were gabbing as they lay in their bunks late at night. Because of Billy's seniority, their cell was located at the end of the block. Two guards happened to be standing in the corridor just around the corner unseen the two men and could not help but hear their conversation.

"How come your wife doesn't come to see you anymore?" Tom asked.

"She's getting old like me - too old to travel far," Billy said sadly. "She has no money, and no one is left alive for her to rely on."

"How long since you last saw her?" Tom asked.

"'bout eight years or so," Billy said.

"A long time," Tom said.

"She still writes me every week," Billy said brightly. "What more can a man ask of his woman, than she has remained faithful to him and has never forgotten him while he serves a life sentence?"

"I'll say." Tom said.

They said nothing for moments. Then, Billy spoke.

"My two wishes, Tom, are that I would like to see my wife, so I could be held in her comforting arms one last time before I die; and I would like to spend one day in normal clothes and out of these prison stripes," Billy said. "When I was a free man, I looked really dapper when I wore my Sunday-go-to-meetin' suit. I'd love to put that look on one last time."

"Not much to ask for a man on the outside, but beyond reason for a lifer, no?" Tom asked.

"Sad to say," Billy said.

"Unless you're plannin' on runnin', your two wishes … well, they won't happen 'til after you die," Tom said. "If your spirit allows, before it goes to your eternal resting place."

"That's how I see my future," Billy said. "I'm too old to run, too slow if I did and wouldn't make 20 miles, let alone 200. Of course, if'n I got the chance to see her for only a day, I'd come right back - 'cause I do owe my debt to society."

The two guards, both about ten years younger than Billy, shook their heads in pity and walked away so they wouldn't be heard.

"That's truly sad," Guard Johnson said. "He has always been a model prisoner. He wouldn't try runnin'. However, if he did, we'd have to shoot him, and that'd be a shame. I'd sure hate doin' that."

"I believe him when he says he would turn himself back in," Guard Crowley said. "He has always been a man of his word."

"Well, we ain't doing nothing to help him," Guard Johnson said. "We'd be fired in a second if we did, and then we'd be joinin' him on the other side of the bars."

No longer overheard by guards, Tom offered Billy an idea.

"If you could get five miles, I have an uncle who could take you the rest of the way," Tom said. "I know he would do it."

85

"If I thought I could git five miles; I might try it," Billy said. "But how could I git away from the bullets and the dogs. It jess won't happen. Jason was talking about running. He'd have a betta chance than me, but I hope he don't try. He don't know his way around dese parts – he'll run his self into quicksand sho' 'nuf."

The next day, in the prison yard, Tom and Jason spoke together in a whisper.

"I heard you might like to try running," Tom said.

"Where'd you hear that?" Jason asked.

"No matter," Tom said. "If you are interested in running with me, I have an uncle who might help us and a way to test our chances."

"Tell me more," Jason said.

They talked in whispers about Tom's plan to talk Billy into running first and then, if he made it, they would have confidence that they too could make. If Billy got caught, then they would drop the idea. Tom ended the conversation with his simple action plan.

"My uncle will find out from Billy how he went through the swamp and then let us know afterwards," Tom said. "If he makes it through."

In October, Carl, the rail gang's trustee died of natural causes. The next time the gang went out to work, the guards made Billy the trustee, because he was now the oldest and the longest serving member. The Boss Man wasn't pleased about it, but he figured Billy posed the least threat of running. As trustee, he was no longer chained to the other prisoners. His job was to bring materials, like spikes and spike clamps, to the prisoners, setup lunch, and haul water to the prisoners and guards. This promotion was long in coming and almost made Billy proud.

One evening in early December, Tom talked to Billy.

"My uncle came to visit me today," Tom said. "I set you up with him. If you can reach his farm, five miles straight north, he will drive you home in his produce truck. He will watch for you sometime this month if you want to try."

"Oh, I don't know if'n I have the nerve," Billy said. "I'd be going agin my beliefs – violatin' my duty to fulfill my sentence."

"What would a day or two out of a life sentence hurt anyone, especially if you came back on your own," Tom said. "Maybe you spend a few days in the box, but you can handle that. You've been there plenty of times."

"Likely, I'd be killed just tryin'," Billy said.

"You're gonna die anyway," Tom said. "At least, least this way you'll have died trying instead'a just wishin'."

"Ya got a bit of logic to what you say," Billy said.

Weeks later at the work site, guards Johnson and Crowley chatted as they watched over the chain gang. They each carried a rifle. The Boss Man went unarmed, leaving the dirty work to his underlings. December had arrived and with it cold, damp air slipping down from up north.

"I heard one of our convicts might be planning a run," Guard Crowley said to Johnson. "Keep your eyes sharp."

"Hope it ain't Billy who's thinkin' it," Guard Johnson said. "He'd be too easy a target."

"If we really tried," Guard Crowley said. Guard Johnson gave him a wink.

Suddenly, a fight broke out between two prisoners, swinging at each other with their sledgehammers and yelling at each other. The Boss Man and the guards ran to break up the disturbance. They waited until the two men wore each other down before stepping in to stop the fracas. When the fight was ended, the Boss Man hollered for Billy to bring him a cup of water. Not hearing a response, the Boss Man turned and saw Billy, in the distance, running with his limp toward the closest wooded swamp. He ran fast for a man his age, with a limp, and had a sizeable lead on his pursuers. Johnson was the closest guard.

"Johnson, shoot that son-of-a-beech," Boss Man shouted.

Johnson took aim, more meticulously than he normally would, so it took a second or two, longer than it might have taken, and then fired. The shot struck the dirt at Billy's feet. The closeness of the bullet put an extra spring in Billy's step, even with the hitch in his stride.

"Damn it, Johnson, you missed," Boss Man shouted. "Take him down!"

Guard Johnson again took careful aim, also a tad more thoroughly than normal, and fired. His shot went high, into the trees. The Boss Man began to suspect that Johnson might be sympathetic to Billy, but he knew he would never be able to prove it. By the time the Boss Man grabbed the gun from Johnson, Billy had entered the swamp and disappeared into the woods.

"Johnson, you and I will be talkin' later," Boss Man shouted. "Crowley, go back, get the dogs and hustle back here pronto with another five men."

Crowley jumped in the truck and barreled off toward the prison.

At the prison, Crowley called out the extra men and, as they loaded kennels on the truck, Crowley fetched the dogs from their pens. He leashed up three large bloodhounds, and, before taking them out to the truck, he found a jar of horse liniment, smeared it on a rag and gave each of the dogs a good whiff. They started sneezing and wheezing. He let them settle down and then took them to the truck, and the men loaded them up. Three of the men jumped in the back of the truck with the kennels while the others piled into the cab, Crowley spun the tires as they rushed off to the work site.

When Crowley and the additional guards arrived back at the work site and unloaded the dogs, the dogs were still occasionally sneezing.

"What's wrong with them dogs?" The Boss Man asked.

"Must be allergies from the road dust," Crowley said.

"They was sneezin' all the way here," one of the other guards said.

Boss man gave Crowley an evil eye but said nothing.

"All right, off with you," he said. "Track him down and don't bunch up in case one of you falls into quicksand. Take a rope with you."

As one guard grabbed a coil of rope from the truck, the posse set out on foot.

At first, the dogs wandered aimlessly across the field, showing no sign of picking up a scent until they finally entered the swamp. Even the dogs seemed to be giving Billy a break.

Billy successfully reached the farm of Tom's uncle, and his uncle was good to his word. He hid Billy under crates of potatoes he was driving to market and drove Billy home -- to see his wife one last time. Billy arrived late at night and was not seen by the neighbors. His neighbors knew him well before he was arrested, could recognize him and might call the sheriff. He couldn't risk being seen.

After hugging and kissing his wife, they talked through the night, reminiscing. The next morning, Billy put on into his old double-breasted suit that his wife had kept dutifully pressed and clean, knowing one day he would need it for his funeral. It hung loose on him, not snug or tight like an old suit would normally hang on a man after twenty-five years. Straightening his tie for him, she thought he looked handsome in it. They spent the morning together, talking, holding hands, and even dancing a little. Christmas was coming, and Billy enjoyed looking at the Christmas tree his wife had put up, as artificial and bedraggled as it was. She had put up the same tree every year since he went away.

The word was on the radio about the jail break and Billy knew the sheriff's deputies would be coming before long to look for him at his wife's house. He considered hiding before they came for him but then he also remembered his pledge to return after a day. She pleaded with him to run with her to another place, but he knew of no other place, had no money; and they were both too tired to run. His dreams were fulfilled.

He could now die happy, having seen his wife one last time. She too realized that their last visit would be as fine an ending to their lives as they could have.

So, Billy and his wife sat down on the living room couch, held hands, looked at the Christmas tree, and awaited the inevitable. After a while, Billy lay down with his head on her lap, gazing at the most beautiful Christmas tree he could recall ever seeing.

Before long, they heard sirens wailing in the distance and knew their time was up.

Finally, with tires screeching, the sheriff's deputies pulled up abruptly in front of Billy's old, dilapidated house. Finding the front door ajar, as Billy liked the fresh air to flow in, the deputies calmly entered without drawing their guns. They knew Billy and expected no resistance from him. As they entered the living room, they saw Billy lying on the couch, his head still in his wife's lap, cradled in her arms.

Her eyes were in tears. His eyes were closed.

Somewhere in the Midwest -- 1987

Sam was getting old. He could feel it in his trembling hands, aching joints, and the shuffle that had replaced his stride. Of all the signs, it was the shuffle that bothered him most. That dragging, defeated gait was the start of the final decline, and he knew it.

He entered the bedroom and opened the top dresser drawer. From beneath a folded doily, he retrieved a silver-plated Glock 9mm pistol. He'd bought it a few years ago in a brief spell of panic after watching a doomsday pundit warn of societal collapse. The world hadn't ended. Not yet.

He turned the gun in his hands until he was staring into the empty void where the clip should be. A few moments of rummaging produced the magazine, and another empty void. No bullets. Reaching farther back, he found a box of ammo. With trembling fingers, he opened it, spilling four rounds into the drawer. He winced, bracing for the clatter on the hardwood bottom. But they landed softly atop his socks.

He picked up one bullet. Just one.

With painstaking care, he loaded it into the clip and then slid the clip into the pistol's handle. He pulled back the slide, chambering the round, and tucked the weapon into the waistband of his pants, concealing it beneath his shirt. Then he shuffled out.

In the kitchen, his wife Betsy stood at the sink, humming as she lowered dishes into soapy water. Rosy-cheeked and round, she looked every bit the cheerful grandmother in her floral-print dress.

She heard the familiar whoosh of his slippers. "Oh, there you are, dear," she said. "Would you mind taking out the garbage?"

Sam opened the cupboard under the sink, retrieved the bag, and shuffled to the sliding glass door. Outside, he dropped the bag into the bin beside the house. Then, without thinking, he grabbed a wooden folding chair leaning against the siding and dragged it, slow and steady, to the yard's edge.

Their house stood alone in the countryside, flanked by fields, and bordered by a quiet stream. There were no neighbors, just silence.

Sam unfolded the chair, sat facing the water, and placed the gun in his lap. He stared at it for a long while, his thoughts drifting between steel and sky, field, and stream. The air was crisp, and the world was still. He raised the pistol to his temple.

A blue jay dropped from the sky and landed in the grass fifteen feet away.

Later, Sam reentered the kitchen.

"That took you long enough," Betsy said, not turning from the sink.

"Damned blue jay was circling the robin's nest again," he muttered, brushing past her.

The pistol remained hidden beneath his shirt. In the bedroom, he locked the safety, removed the clip, ejected one bullet, and returned everything to the drawer. Casually but carefully, he added a layer of socks on top.

Two months passed.

This time, he returned to the drawer with intention, loaded the gun, and tucked it beneath his shirt.

Only he noticed the difference, the shuffle had slowed.

As Betsy sat at the kitchen table snapping beans for dinner, he said, "I'm going to check if the robin chicks have flown."

"That's nice, dear."

Outside, the chair was still there, waiting. Sam brushed away a few dead leaves, sat down, and rested the gun on his lap. Again, the landscape caught his attention. Again, he lifted the gun to his head.

A frog croaked from somewhere in the stream.

Later, Betsy looked up from the table. "Any chicks in the nest?"

"No," he said. "Just frogs."

She turned to glance at him. "Frogs in a bird's nest?" But she said nothing more.

In the bedroom, Sam checked the safety, put the gun away, and sat on the bed, tears brimming.

Three months later, he returned to the drawer once more. This time, he was using a cane.

As he shuffled to the sliding door, Betsy said, "Are you Checking for frogs in the robin's nest?"

Sam didn't answer.

He reached the chair. Sat. Rested the pistol on his lap. This time, he didn't look away.

He raised the gun.

A pheasant shrieked somewhere in the field.

Inside, Betsy placed the last dish into the cupboard. A sound reached her, a sound that cracked the quiet.

A gunshot.

Frozen, then moving fast, she rushed to the door. Fumbled it open. Stepped outside.

There was Sam, shuffling slowly toward the house, gun in hand, smoke curling from the barrel.

"Damn pheasant," he muttered as he passed her.

She stared, speechless, as he disappeared into the house.

In the bedroom, Sam removed the clip and threw it and the gun into the drawer. He sat heavily on the bed, tears streaking his face.

Then he lay down, turned toward the wall, and waited for the inevitable.

Chicago -- 1995

In a small urban apartment, sitting across the kitchen table from Sam Johnson, Jake Johnson fumed.

"We're gonna kill him," Jake said. "End of story."

Twenty-something brothers from the streets of Chicago's north side, their street-hardness showed in their look, their black stovepipe jeans, their thin-cut beards, and their arrogance. Paulo Ramirez, a short Mexican, sitting over in the corner with his chair tipped against the wall, topped off the trio. Paulo, two years younger than the brothers, wore a ring in one ear. His head was shaved and tattoos covered both arms.

"What do you mean, we?" Sam shot back.

"What if he's innocent?" Paulo asked.

"Oh, Ritter's the one, all right," Jake said. "Willy and Tom were both there and they told me what happened."

"Tom and Willy? You listened to them?" Paulo asked. "What if your cousin started the fight?" Jake slammed his fist on the table, stood up and paced around the room.

"What if he did?" Jake asked. "It still isn't right that Ritter killed him."

"What about the law?" Sam asked. "They'll give Ritter the chair or the needle, or wait, do they still hang people in Illinois?"

"You're a fool if you think the state doles out justice," Jake said. "His case will be dropped on a technicality or dismissed by some well-paid lawyer's bullshit defense. This is about family honor, and family is ultimately responsible for delivering justice for the family."

"Spoken like a true Jihadist," Paulo said.

"That's an eye for an eye, right?' Sam said. "Even in Arab countries, I don't think anyone takes an eye for an eye anymore.

"I'll bet they don't punish rape with rape." Paulo said.

Jake sat down again. They sat in silence for a few minutes.

"Wouldn't a long, miserable life in prison serve as a better punishment than a quick and painless death?" Sam asked.

"I like that suggestion," Jake said. "I can kill him slowly - that would help the family feel better."

"Wouldn't putting him away for the rest of his miserable life make the family feel even better, and for far longer?" Sam asked.

"It's not the same." Jake said. "What if he escaped?"

"The law would catch him and put him back,' Paulo said. "Escapees always get recaptured around here."

"If they didn't catch him again, then you could hunt him down," Sam said.

Jake rose to his feet without answering and left the room; the others followed him into the dining room.

"Where's dad's Ruger?" Jake asked.

"That old piece of junk — probably doesn't even fire anymore," Sam said.

Jake rifled the contents of the top cupboard drawer until he found the silver automatic pistol and removed the clip. He worked the action twice; everything seemed in working order.

"When one person murders another and becomes a danger to the public, society has the right, the obligation, no, the duty, to remove that killer from our midst – permanently, and I'm the member of society who is going to remove Ritter," Jake said, as he found a box of bullets and began loading the clip.

"Yeah, but society is supposed to dispense justice without emotion or anger," Paulo said. "It's supposed to be deliberate and objective."

"Where'd you hear that?" Jake asked.

"Civics class, in school," Paulo said.

"Shit, you don't even attend school anymore," Jake said. "What do you know?"

"Paulo was a decent student before he had to drop out. Still remembers the good stuff, right?" Sam asked.

"Well, screw that," Jake said. "It's simple to me. You can't let killers get away with killing. Kill half a dozen of them and, before long, others will be afraid to follow in their footsteps." Everyone let that sink in.

"Ah, the old deterrent argument," Sam said.

"When the threats of getting caught and being punished are removed, criminals do swarm," Paulo said. "Even decent folks turn criminal when the rules vanish, remember the looting after Katrina?" Governors always turn out their National Guard troops when a disaster occurs to prevent looting. Otherwise, law-abiding people turn into animals in the absence of law enforcement."

"Yeah!" Jake said, appreciating the support.

"The death penalty has stopped so many killings, right?" Sam asked. "That's why the murder rate in the U.S. is the highest among the major countries in the world."

"Is that sarcasm?" Paulo asked. English was his second language.

"Well, this American is eradicating one killer," Jake said.

"By doing what, another killing?" Sam retorted. "Where does the cycle end? Will his relatives come after you? Why couldn't life in prison, assuming the prison is miserably uncomfortable, be enough?"

"What's miserable about our prison system?" Jake asked. "U.S. prisons are like cheap country clubs."

"Well, that would have to change if the death penalty went away," Sam said. "I'm not saying dungeons and the rack. I'm saying bland existence. No television, no movies, no entertainment, no cigarettes, no privileges. Boring food, no visits - from anyone. They could have a set of classic philosophy books to read, to educate them about why they did what they did, and perhaps a bible, so they can repent before they die. That's it."

"That would be one crappy existence, and they'd have a whole lifetime to reflect on where they went wrong," Paulo said.

"Exactly," Sam said.

"Crappy existence prison will never happen," Jake said. "Congress has too much empathy for human rights and not enough for victim rights."

Jake headed for the door, motioning for the others to follow.

"When you think of the number of people sentenced to die each year, how long it takes each execution to happen, and the handful of killers put to death each year, how much of a deterrent can the death penalty be?" Paulo asked.

"Police detectives will tell you that capital crimes are committed primarily by men under the age of thirty, on alcohol, drugs or with demented minds. People like that don't think about consequences, let alone the death penalty," Sam said.

"You both are overthinking this," Jake said. "It's best if I lay down the law myself. Let's go."

They walked out the door and toward Jake's '82 black Mustang GT, parked on the street in front of Sam and Jake's house. Paulo squeezed into the back seat while Sam slid into the "shotgun" seat. Being after 11:00 PM, with no moon above and dim streetlamps, the city was dark.

Jake started the engine, pulled the shifter into first gear, and peeled away from the curb.

"I've heard that the death penalty is unfairly applied too, at times," Sam said.

"Especially for us minorities," Paulo said.

"Heck, Hispanics are hardly a minority anymore," Jake said. "And nothing about life is fair."

"Think about it: the worst murderers are often not the ones executed. Take Ted Kaczynski, Terry Nichols, O.J. Simpson and Andrea Yates, to name four," Sam said.

"That's because they had the best attorneys, the big publicity-hounds," Paulo said, "while the poor nobody-killers suffer from the incompetence of greenhorn public defenders."

"That's another reason for taking care of this business myself," Jake said.

They turned onto Addison St, headed east. And picked up speed.

"Don't forget the human element," Sam said. "Detectives, evidence lab technicians, defense attorneys, judges, and juries – they're all human and humans make mistakes. Poor, innocent defendants don't have a prayer."

They turned north on Clark St., where the streetlights and business signs were bright, and slowed down when they saw a Chicago Police car approaching from ahead.

"Well, I'm not taking the chance of Ritter beating the rap through a technicality, a prosecuting attorney mistake or an incompetent judge," Jake said. "I'm keeping matters in my own hands - keeping it simple."

"You're missing the point," Sam said. "I'm saying that if you let the legal system handle this, that a life sentence of miserable existence is better than the death penalty, because it could always be reversed, in those cases when the system failed, and the mistake uncovered. And, if no mistake has been made, the guilty will suffer a long time."

"If just one innocent person is executed," Paulo said, "the death penalty shouldn't be used on anyone. Wouldn't you agree? Especially if that one person is you."

The Mustang turned down a quiet side street. The neighborhood was older now, with boarded-up windows, cracked sidewalks, and the occasional dog barking somewhere out of sight.

"That could apply to you, Jake," Sam said quietly. "What if you're wrong about Ritter? Or even if you're right, if the law doesn't see it your way? What if you kill him, get caught, and end up on trial yourself? Then you're facing judgment, and this system you don't trust is your only way out."

Jake stared ahead through the windshield, his hands rigid on the wheel. He didn't answer.

"You want justice," Paulo added, "but you also want to live. And you don't strike me as the kind of guy who wants to rot in a cell or die in one of those concrete bunkers downstate."

No word from Jake. He turned another corner, the engine in low and steady.

"Think about it," Sam pressed. "You're the one who said Ritter doesn't deserve to live. Fine. Then let the courts bury him alive, let him die slowly in a cell, forgotten. You want him to suffer? That's the way. This other way? You could suffer too. You just don't know it yet."

The car rolled to a stop in front of a shadowy block. Jake sat for a moment, motionless. A beat-up sedan passed behind them and honked once before continuing. Jake pulled into an alley, paused, then slowly backed out.
"I don't know what to think anymore," he muttered. "Let's go home. We'll call the cops. Let them deal with Ritter."

San Francisco -- 1980

Outside, the spring morning was warm, and I was trying to enjoy a rare moment of silence. But my mind wouldn't cooperate. It bounced between three thoughts: how old and worn my precinct, bullpen, and desk had become; how a hybrid British-Chinese guy like me ended up a detective in an American police station; and what I ought to have for lunch. That's when the phone jangled.

"Chinatown precinct, Rogers here," I said.

On the other end of the phone, the desk sergeant downstairs mumbled, "A routine murder over on Beckett Street. A woman witness is standing by with the beat patrolman."

He didn't tell me the building number, but Beckett Street is only a block long. I figured I could find the pair by sight. As I rose to leave, *no murder is routine,* especially in San Francisco's Chinatown in the middle of the twentieth century. *I'll straighten the sergeant out on that later.*

I reached the scene in minutes. Police barriers and yellow tape cordoned off a forty-foot semi-circle around the open door of a well-known Chinese restaurant. In the center of the semi-circle lay the crumpled body of a man, a dark pool of blood outlining him like a shadow. Two patrolmen stood like sentries, waiting for my grand entrance. My partner was off exploring the deserts of Utah on vacation, so I was the Lone Ranger on this one, riding in without Tonto.

The patrolman and a woman stood just outside the tape, exactly where they should have been.

"Mrs. Wong, meet Detective Rogers," the patrolman said. "Detective, the man on the sidewalk is Long Chuo." Then he stepped back, surprising me with his formality and politeness.

Mrs. Wong was Chinese, in her early fifties, and reached about my shoulder. She wore the obligatory black dress of a widow, though she seemed too young for the role. She was stoically calm, like someone who'd seen violent death before.

"Mrs. Wong, did you see what happened? And if so, can you describe it?" I asked.

"I was on my way to meet my uncle for lunch at the Flying Dragon, just beyond this restaurant, when a young man standing on the sidewalk suddenly shot and killed that man in the doorway," she said.

"Can you describe the young man?" I asked.

"Yes," she said. "He was two to three inches shorter than you, perhaps five-foot-ten, in his twenties, black hair, shirtless, with blue work pants and running shoes."

"Chinese?"

"Yes."

"Would you recognize him if you saw him again?"

"Of course. He wore no shirt and had a colorful bird tattoo across his back, from shoulder to shoulder."

"So he was facing away from you."

"At first, when he was shooting. After the man went down, he turned to face me, backed down the street to the corner, and then ran."

"Did he threaten to shoot you?"

"No. He looked right at me as if looking through me."

"How many shots?"

"Three. Of that, I am positive."

The patrolman returned.

"I just heard that Patrolman Chang, over on Jackson, stopped a man he saw ditching a .38 in a trash can. He's holding him now."

"Was he shirtless?"

"Don't know," he said. "I'll borrow your car radio and find out."

"Ask him to take the suspect to the station and have Sergeant Wu arrange a line-up. Then escort Mrs. Wong down there and have her wait at my desk. I'll be right behind you."

I turned to Mrs. Wong. "Would you be willing to go with the officer to the station? We'll need an hour or two of your time."

"Let me tell my uncle I won't be having lunch with him," she said.

"Stay with her, officer."

I walked over to inspect the body. The coroner had just arrived and was outlining the body with chalk, avoiding the pooled blood. The victim was an older Chinese man, who appeared to have died instantly and collapsed onto his right side, facing the street.

"Looks like two bullet holes," the coroner said. "Both went completely through. Undoubtedly large caliber and probably metal-jacketed."

Perhaps Mrs. Wong had miscounted, I thought. At such close range, the shooter shouldn't have missed, unless the man had dropped in the midst of the shots being fired.

"Odd," the coroner said. "The stippling is irregular. How close was the shooter?"

Close, I thought.

107

"I'll clarify that at the station." I said.

I inspected the rest of the scene. I found no shell casings, which meant the shooter's gun must have been a revolver or the shooter had picked up his casings.

When I arrived at the office, Mrs. Wong was patiently waiting and the polite patrolman had remained with her – easier duty than walking his beat, I figured.

"Her uncle had left the restaurant, so we came straight here," he said.

"Is the line-up ready?" I asked.

"The Sergeant Wu just called," he said.

We went downstairs to the viewing room adjacent to the line-up room. Six shirtless Chinese men of different builds were lined up, each close to five-foot-ten, and visible through the one-way mirror. I wondered how many were patrolmen, probably most, given the short notice. I find it ironic how often policemen, filling in a line-up, look like criminals.

"Mrs. Wong, do you recognize the shooter?" I asked.

"Could you ask them to turn around?" she asked.

When they turned, I was surprised to see that none of them had a tattoo on his back.

"Oh dear," she said. "Turn them around again."

When they turned back to face the mirror, she hesitated. "He looked like number four, but with no tattoo, he can't be the man I saw."

"Hold number four over the intercom," I said, knowing he was the one who the patrolman say ditch the pistol, uncertain whether we had the shooter or not. I began to realize that this case would not be closed quickly.

As we returned to my desk, I asked Mrs. Wong, "When the suspect was firing his gun, how close was he standing to the victim?

She thought for a moment and then answered, "Less than six feet, I'd say."

"And the victim was facing the shooter, right?" I asked.

Most certainly," she said. "I saw him fall – onto his right side."

She was starting to cry.

"That will do, for now," I said. "The officer will take you home now."

I could only hold the suspect for forty-eight hours unless the test results came back from the lab matching his gun to the slugs that went through the victim. We also were checking Gunshot Residue from his hands. Unfortunately, we hadn't found the slugs yet. Even if we had to release him, at least we would know who he was. Number four was a street-level drug dealer and extortionist named Billy Yee. The victim was a local wholesale food salesman named Lang Tong, with no criminal record. The facts were just not adding up, so the next morning, I returned to the scene.

The barricades were gone, the body was gone, and even the blood pool was gone – business appeared to be back to normal on Beckett Street. As I stood in the doorway, my eyes were drawn to a shadow on the sidewalk – the outline of a large bird. Looking up, I saw the sign extending from the building, showing the name of the restaurant, the Golden Pheasant. At the end of the arm holding the sign hung the figure of a pheasant in colorful stained glass. With sunlight through the glass at just the right angle, the shadow could look like a tattoo, especially if Yee was standing in the perfect place, where the shadow would fall neatly on his back. We had the right man after all. However, I still could not explain two bullet holes and three shots fired. I needed to find the slugs.

Entering the restaurant, I was greeted by a young man who introduced himself as the manager, Mr. Guang. He was thin and tall with a narrow face. He struck me as being too young to be the owner. Since the majority of restaurants in Chinatown are family-owned and have been in the same families for years, I suspected an elder relative was silently operating behind this manager.

"Is your father available?" I asked, making a blind assumption.

"Uh, why, umm," he stammered, "he's ill, in bed. Can I help you?"

"I'm Detective Rogers, investigating the murder in your doorway yesterday."

"Just horrible," he said, looking at the empty tables. "And bad for business."

I walked around the restaurant looking for slugs and bullet holes, since two had passed through the body and one, apparently, missed. "Have you swept the restaurant since the shooting?" I asked.

"I don't think so," he said. "Cleaning up the doorway took a long time."

I found no spent slugs in the dining room. Across the back of the restaurant stood a seven- foot-tall, twelve-feet-wide, intricate, hand-carved rosewood screen. I saw no bullet holes in the screen's wood -- but it was full of openings through which a slug easily could have passed. Behind the screen was the opening to the kitchen, wide enough for two waiters to pass without colliding, and easy enough for a bullet to continue its path into the kitchen. Inspecting the back wall of the kitchen, the last stop north for any bullets from the entrance, I found no bullet holes again. Where did the slugs end up?

I returned to my office and learned that the victim had been shot in the back with a .45 caliber metal-cased bullet and that only one shot had been fired from the gun retrieved from our only suspect. That news turned my theory upside down. The suspect must have been shooting at a target inside the restaurant and the person in the restaurant must have been shooting back at the suspect. So, who had fired from inside the restaurant? I sent a patrolman to search for spent slugs across the street from the restaurant. As I'd hoped, he found two .45-caliber slugs embedded in the wall of the opposite building. My theory shifted: our suspect had exchanged shots with someone inside the restaurant, and the victim was caught in the crossfire. I headed back to the scene to find out who had been inside at the time of the shooting.

This time, I returned with a search warrant, not knowing who might have shot the victim. I brought three officers with me to conduct a thorough search. As soon as we entered the kitchen, five Chinese cooks began shouting, waving knives and cleavers, and generally acting belligerent. We held our ground, flashing our badges and keeping our hands near our weapons, but they refused to cooperate.

Once we established control and began searching the kitchen, we found a .45-caliber pistol and two casings hidden in the cooler, buried in a case of bok choy. The shooter had picked up his casings, so we knew the weapon had to be semi-

111

automatic. From the number of rounds left in the clip and the two recovered casings, I could tell the gun had been fired twice.

Returning to the restaurant manager, I asked him, "Tell me what happened here yesterday."

He didn't answer me.

"Test his hands for gunshot residue," I said to the lab technician who had accompanied me. In minutes, I was informed that the test was negative. The manager probably didn't fire the gun.

I went to my car and radioed a request back to the station to dispatch Inspector Yu, another detective in our precinct who spoke fluent Chinese. My mother spoke to me in Chinese, as a child, but I wanted to become an American and always answered in English.

When Inspector Yu arrived, I asked him to interview the boisterous kitchen staff. In the end, the interviews were conflicting – some saying a man came in from the alley and others saying no one came through the kitchen. I suspected some were intentionally misleading us – out of misguided loyalty to their owner and his family, fear of having to testify, or to protect their jobs. Sick or not, the father was my next stop.

"Mr. Guang, where is your father?" I asked. "I must speak with him."

"He is ill and should not be disturbed," he said.

"This is not a request," I said. "I must insist under our court order."

He hesitated, then finally said, "He's upstairs." I waved to the nearest patrolman to follow. Reluctantly, the son led us out the kitchen's back door and to a narrow passageway between his restaurant and the Flying Dragon next door. A staircase inside led to an upstairs apartment.

He knocked softly, then pushed the door open. A worried older woman greeted us. After a brief exchange with her son, she led us to a rear bedroom.

We found the father, old, pale, gray-haired, lying on a small, low bed. A quilt covered him up to the chin. Beads of perspiration dotted his forehead. His eyes were closed as if he were saving his strength to fight off whatever illness plagued him. I approached the bed with respect.

"What is his illness?" I asked.

"He has the flu," the son said.

I turned to leave when I noticed a pair of scissors on the bed table -- the style that has a flat dull blade on one side, used for cutting under bandages. Of what use would such scissors be in treating the flu? I reached down and gently pulled back the quilt, exposing a bandaged shoulder with blood seepage. He gradually opened his eyes and looked wearily at me.

"You've been shot," I said, glancing at the son and mother. Then I motioned for the son to follow me out of the room.

"He needs to be in a hospital, and you and I need to talk." I sent the officer downstairs to call an ambulance.

"You didn't take him in because you knew gunshot wounds get reported. But in doing that, you may have put your father's life in danger. Now, tell me what happened."

The son hesitated.

"When they remove the bullet from his shoulder," I said, "we'll know which gun it came from. And that might point the murder charge at your father. So I need the truth, now."

113

"He didn't shoot anyone," he shouted. "Okay? Some stranger ran in from the alley, started firing at the man on the sidewalk, Mr. Tong and, when the man outside shot back, he hit my father. The stranger ran out the same way he entered. He must have dropped the gun as he ran out. A cook must have seen the gun lying near my father and decided he needed to help my father by hiding the gun in the cooler.

"S "So why didn't you explain this to the police when it happened?" I asked.

"Drug lords and gangs selling protection surround us," he said. "We cannot risk angering them."

"If you never report them, the extortion will never stop," I said. "Did you recognize the 'stranger,' as you called him?"

I watched closely for any sign of deception or hesitation but saw none.

"No," he said.

"Can you describe him?" I asked.

"Middle-aged, short and stocky, with salt-and-pepper hair."

"Any tattoos or other identifying marks?"

"None that I noticed," he said.

Once again, the case had reached a dead end. The suspect in custody wasn't likely to cooperate, and I had no leverage to compel him. His story of self-defense would hold, for now.

The so-called *stranger's* path was retraced, starting at the kitchen's back door, trying to determine his point of entry and exit. I walked up and down the alley, letting the rhythm of movement stir a new theory from the tangle of conflicting thoughts. Eventually, the trail led me back to the office, this time with a hint of direction.

Back at the station, I sent a patrolman to bring Mrs. Wong in again and asked her to bring the uncle she had planned to meet for lunch. Maybe he had seen the stranger, I told her. I also asked Sergeant Wu for another favor: to bring some mug books of known drug dealers. Perhaps they could identify the assailant among the usual suspects.

When Mrs. Wong and her uncle, Mr. Jin Wong, arrived, I escorted them to an interview room and explained that we were looking for a man seen fleeing the Chinese Pheasant restaurant. Jin Wong looked in his sixties, with thinning hair and a thick midsection, but he also looked mean.

When Sergeant Wu entered the room carrying the mug shot books, he stopped in his tracks, backed out quickly, and waved me into the hallway.

"What's wrong?" I asked.

"That man is in this mug book right here," he said.

"Oh really," I said, only slightly surprised.

"He's a suspected drug dealer," Wu said. "They've tried but haven't been able to pin anything on Jin Wong. He's been pulled in on at least half a dozen cases where others named him, but he always had an alibi."

"Let me have the remaining mug books, Sergeant, hold onto the one with Jin Wong's photo. I need to keep them busy," I said. "And then send up a lab tech with a gunshot residue kit."

I returned to the room, laid the mug books on the table and asked Mrs. Wong and her uncle to look through the books to see if they recognized anyone from the time of the murder, knowing full well the uncle wouldn't pick out anyone, and expecting that Mrs. Wong hadn't seen anyone but the shooter and the victim.

The lab tech arrived, and I explained to the Wongs that we were routinely testing everyone who was near the crime scene. At first the uncle resisted, claiming he owned registered guns and had fired several recently.

"I'll note that," I said. That seemed to calm him down. I also suspected he knew he had washed his hands well after the shooting. As I expected, the test showed only slight traces on his right hand and none on hers. I asked them to continue looking through the mug books, as Sergeant Wu brought in more. Then I stepped out of the room with the Sergeant and sent him on another mission while I returned to the room.

I stalled for time, asking them questions as they flipped through the books. I asked the uncle why he wasn't there when his niece arrived late for their lunch. He said he had forgotten that he had another important business appointment and had to leave abruptly. He said the commotion must have happened after he left. I also asked him if he had seen any strangers in the restaurant where he had been waiting, the Flying Dragon, who might have slipped out the back door. He was becoming nervous and continued to claim he didn't recognize anyone in the mug books. I kept him busy with inane questions, to which the uncle's answers continued to be either vague or unhelpful, until I heard a knock at the interview room door.

At that point I rose from my chair and then stood back as I opened the door wide. Standing outside were the five cooks from the restaurant. They instantly exploded into gesticulations, shouting, pointing, and threatening.

"I'll accept that as a positive identification, Inspector," I said, as I closed the door.

"He will be taking their statements now," I said to Mr. Wong. The niece looked at her uncle in shock and anger.

"You?" she asked. "How could you?"

"How do you think I took care of you and your mother over the years after your father died?" Mr. Wong asked.

"Take him away," I said to the nearest patrolman. "We are charging him with the attempted murder of Billy Yee and second-degree murder for killing Long Chuo, the man caught in the crossfire on the sidewalk."

From that point on, the case proceeded quickly to its conclusion. The sidewalk suspect, Billy Yee, rolled over on Mr. Wong, as soon as he heard Wong was under arrest and that we had other corroborating witnesses, and because he didn't want to be charged as an accessory. For assault with a deadly weapon and a reduced drug sentence, Billy Yee's attorney plea-bargained his sentence down to eight years in state prison.

For second degree murder, attempted murder, and dealing drugs, which we found searching his apartment, Mr. Wang received eighteen years to life. His niece never spoke to him again.

Mr. Guang recovered from his shoulder wound and added his identification of the stranger to those of the cooks. His son, who we could have charged with obstruction, wasn't prosecuted, because a jury would be sympathetic to him protecting his family.

Case closed. Justice served, this time, at least. I headed back to my desk to let the silence settle back in, and to remind the desk sergeant that no murder is ever routine.

ASSISTANT DEPUTY SHERIFF OF CURRITUCK COUNTY

Currituck County, North Carolina -- 1962

I was dozing in my front porch rocking chair on a warm summer morning when Buddy Lawson jolted me awake by bounding up my front steps two at a time, shouting breathlessly, "Deputy! I've been burgled -- my money's gone, and my merchandise is scattered around."

Buddy, a five-foot-six, gray-haired, rotund native North Carolinian, perpetually in bib overalls, owned the general store, the only store in our tiny community.

Crimes were as rare as Yankees in our part of the County, where I served as deputy sheriff. The people who lived there were poor, and Buddy had been known to keep families afloat by extending credit for food, even when he knew full well, he'd never collect. That was the kind of man he was, and I hated to hear trouble had come his way.

"How much was taken?" I asked.

"Three hundert dollars," Buddy said. "My bank payment, and I'm already behind. The bank'll take my store for sure. If my money's gone, I'm ruined."

"That'd hurt every family in our community. The next closest store's fifty miles away, and lots of folks still get around by horseback," I said. "Seen Jocko?" I asked, hoping to distract him.

Jocko was my black mongrel, a dog with a personal sense of justice. By day, he was placid, downright friendly to locals, and could usually be found sleeping in the cool shade of the old live oak tree in front of Buddy's store. But when night fell, he came alive. He'd patrol the town on his own terms,

119

enforcing his own idea of the law. I hadn't seen him since the night before and was starting to worry.

"Jocko's under his tree," Buddy said.

I accompanied Buddy back to his store, an old, weather-worn, lap-sided building with a wide front porch cluttered with various sale items, a barrel of fishin' poles, a stack of oil cans, and one new power lawn mower, his entire inventory of mowers. Lawns were scarce around here, so demand for power mowers was limited, especially since most locals had more time than money to spend on conveniences.

Buddy was an industrious soul. He'd taken over an abandoned house about ten years back and, through his own labor, turned it into the part-store, part-home that stood before me. He lived alone above the store. Though meager, the store was central to our community, vital to residents scattered across the county in ramshackle homes.

Most folks earned their living running crabbing boats on Albemarle Sound or net-trolling along our coast. Others traveled inland on farm-owned trucks to labor on cotton or peanut farms. Motorized conveniences like power mowers were rare. And as hard as life was here, burglary had been unheard of, at least since I had taken the job ten years ago. Citizens were religious and accordingly honest folk. Until now.

As we approached the porch steps, I saw coffee cans, candy bars, packs of Lucky Strikes, and pouches of chewing tobacco scattered across the ground and porch. Jocko sat calmly beneath the oak, alert and watching the scene. Inside, the point of entry was obvious, a window had been left unlocked. It was still open, and the panes were unbroken.

While I inspected the store, a wiry local named Ralph Orison ran in through the doorway. He was jockey-sized, but the dark skin on his face and arms showed wear beyond his forty-some years.

"Sheriff, I heard about the break-in," he said, panting. "Thought you should know, there's a pickup parked in that peach grove next to the Johnson place."

After checking the empty cash register, I walked the half mile to Johnson's orchard.

Parked among the trees, I found a beat-up '48 Ford with the keys still in the ignition. In its heyday, it had been fire-engine red, but now it was closer to a dusty rose. Around the driver's side, I saw numerous footprints, a dozen cigarette butts, and on the passenger side, more tracks, and a discarded Hershey bar wrapper. Looked like two men had been waiting there, likely until Buddy closed for the night.

I returned to the store, and as I climbed the porch stairs, I spotted a car parked on the shady side. Inside, Ralph and Buddy sat silently while a stranger in a humidity-rumpled suit and narrow gray tie talked at them, not with them. Unusual duds for our part of the world, especially on a ninety-degree day.

"This here's Mr. Milton from the bank," Buddy said. "He's come for payment or to take possession of my store. What am I to do?"

"Mr. Milton, I'm afraid you can't take possession of the store while it's a crime scene," I said.

That was not strictly true, but I hoped he would not know the difference. Evidently, he did not. But he gave me the iciest glare I ever saw.

"I'll return tomorrow," he said. "And I'll bring your boss, the sheriff, just to make sure the transfer happens smoothly."

I ignored the threat, maybe foolishly. As he left, I heard a low growl rumbling up from Jocko. Apparently, he did not like the banker either.

"Buddy, do you remember anything unusual about your customers yesterday?" I asked.

"Well, I'm a tad foggy about yesterday, but, in the mornin', Mrs. Johnson bought three yards of gingham," he said.

"No, I mean anyone out of the ordinary."

"Oh, I recalls two good ole boys," Buddy said. "My guess is they was from out west, by the Alleghenies."

"Why d'you think they came from there?"

"Well, they talked a bit different, had a working truck, and money to waste on a candy bar," Buddy answered.

"Deputy," Ralph said, "if that truck over by the Johnsons' is theirs, where'd the culprits disappear to?"

"Let's try to reconstruct this," I said. "They came in during the day and likely cased the place. Probably noticed Buddy's register full of cash, and maybe him takin' a nip from that bottle behind the counter."

"Well, life ain't been too rosy lately," Buddy said, a bit defensive. "What with the bank after my home and store."

"They likely figured he'd sleep soundly. So they unlatched a window, came back after dark, grabbed the cash, rummaged through the store for more, and left out the front door. But they didn't make it back to their truck. No blood, no bodies, so they must still be nearby. Let's check for tracks in another direction."

I stepped outside, Buddy and Ralph trailing me, and walked a circle around the building. Too many folks had come and gone, no usable footprints. I considered seeing if Jocko could track them, but he had never shown much bloodhound talent.

From the porch, I studied the trail of scattered goods and noticed a pattern.

"Something happened near the tree," I said, sweeping my arm. "The trail's mostly here."

Still followed by Buddy and Ralph, I approached the oak where Jocko sat. He wore a look I rarely saw on him during daylight, pride. He was sitting up, alert, not dozing as usual.

"Look up," I said.

There, high as two men could climb, crouched the burglars, hiding in the branches.

"Come on down from there!" I hollered. "We can see you!"

"We ain't comin' down 'til you put that dog away," one hollered back.

"Jocko, go on home," I said, pointing. He started off slowly, pausing every few steps to look back.

"We'll wait 'til he's outta sight," one of them called.

Turned out Jocko had found them in the dark, run them up the tree, and kept them there all night, silent as a shadow.

Buddy got his three hundred dollars back, made his bank payment, cut back on his drinking, and started locking up

123

nightly. The northeast corner of Currituck County returned to its peaceful ways.

I went back to my front porch rocking chair, and Jocko reclaimed his shady spot beneath the oak.

Everything returned to normal.

San Francisco -- 1870

I have dreaded revealing what happened to me ten years ago, but now I must. I have never mentioned this to anyone until now. Since I am to be married in two weeks, and my wife will ask about the countless small scars covering my body, I must be prepared to tell her. I have decided to tell you what happened first. My hope is that, when the time comes to tell my soon-to-be-wife, the second telling will go easier on my psyche. If I can be composed in telling her about my past, I hope her reactions will be softened.

To reflect for even an instant on the origin of my scars, let alone recounting the entire ordeal, raises, from deep within my soul, glass-sharp memories of pain. I hoped to put off any retelling forever, but alas, I cannot. Only true love could force me to dredge up this buried portion of my life - my former life.

I was not always the model citizen I am today. I was evil to my core. About twenty years ago, while in my late twenties, I fell into fast company and easy money. Before long, I became the leader of a gang. I am not blaming anyone or anything for my past behavior, as I always was more than a willing participant. Accepting responsibility for my decisions is one of many principles I learned through my experiences.

My main evil was smuggling opium from China through a remote island in the South Seas to San Francisco, for distribution to the extensive Chinese Laborer population resident there. Their proclivity for opium provided a ready market for my product. I led a network of intermediate buyers who were well-known locally and could travel easily among their community.

America's Civil War was raging at the time - a time when most men my age were engaged in America's greatest battle for survival as a nation. While one side fought to separate the country into two lesser countries, and the other fought to unite two opposing factions into one greater country, I stayed out of the fray and pursued my own greedy purposes. As a British citizen with no real stake in who won, I turned my attention instead to acquiring whatever I could, not out of any grand ambition or desire for status, but simply because I wanted more. It was not noble, and I knew it. At some point, I stopped noticing who might be getting hurt along the way.

As I said, my operation was centered on a tiny, nameless, remote island in the middle of the Pacific. I operated in this corner of the world because the island lacked any form of government and because its residents were descendants of pirates, and therefore, lacked common mores. On the island, my operation received inbound shipments from disparate Far East origins and assembled them into larger batches for transport to San Francisco and delivery to my distributors.

My troubles began on a routine visit to the island to pick up my next consignment. The inbound shipments had been delayed, and I was anxious about delivering my product on time. To meet the timetable arranged with my distributors in San Francisco, my ship had to set sail on the next day's first high tide. The evening before we were set to leave, I was restless, partly from the delays encountered, partly from the on-going risk of being attacked by other islanders as ruthless as I was, and partly from the ominous nature of the weather. Tidal waves of dark, thick clouds rolled across the sky, signaling a stormy night. While anxious about these possibilities, an unexplainable, vague apprehension roiled my body and disturbed my mind. I retired early anticipating a restless night.

During the night, the island's residents fell under the heavy hand of the gods. Lightening crashed randomly across the island. One bolt hit a palm tree fifty feet away, exploding it and sending coconuts and palm fronds flying in my direction. Rain pelted the thatched roof of the hut where I was trying to sleep, and the wind blew rain sideways into the interior, as my hut was open on two sides. The rain was warm but cloying in the humidity and sweltering heat. I adapted by stringing up my hammock in the only barely-sheltered corner on the leeward side of my hut. Winds roared, drowning the night's sounds, and the torrential rain blocked out every sight. I felt as alone that night as anyone could anywhere in the world. However, I was not.

As I crawled under the mosquito netting and into my swinging hammock, I could hear the sound of a marauding night insect, which apparently had taken shelter in my hut. The sound was louder than a common mosquito, akin to the buzz of a June bug or a small beetle. I could not see it but distinctly heard it land, close to my head. Confident that I was protected by the netting, any concerns passed quickly from my mind.

Before long, as I lay on my left side, I was drifting between sleep and wakefulness – riding along in that cloudy condition where dreams begin to slip in, and the problems of the day begin to slip out. Suddenly, I felt the bug walking from where my cheek meets my earlobe, up into my ear. The bug moved directly into my ear canal. I felt its tiny feet trudging into the outer entrance of my ear canal and into the channel toward my eardrum. In my stupefied state, I slapped at it, hoping to foil its advance.

As swiftly as my brain could send a signal to the muscles of my arm, ordering it to raise my arm to my head and my hand to my ear, I was too late. Inserting the tip of my finger into my ear, I was unable to stop the bug's progress or to dig it out as it marched deep into my ear canal.

Horrified, I awaited the consequences. I expected the bug to bite me or worse , start nesting, lay eggs that would hatch into resident offspring. I imagined an entire family feeding on the soft tissues of my inner ear before emerging as adults to fly off and find another victim. Not wanting this outcome, I jumped up and pulled a straw from the interior of my hut's roof. At first, I hesitated to poke a stick into my ear canal, worried that I might puncture my eardrum before touching the bug. I also hesitated at poking it with the straw, as doing so might cause it to bite. Or, worse, I might kill it and then be unable to extract its carcass - only to have its body fester and infect my ear and possibly my brain. It would be weeks before I would reach San Francisco and find a doctor with the skills and tools to remove this foreign object from my ear. However, I could not stand the feeling of its presence, so I carefully and gently probed my ear canal to see if I could encourage it to leave. I failed. The straw did not seem to touch it, even though I probed as deeply as I dared. I could sense through the nerves in my ear canal that the bug remained firmly entrenched. I also tried flushing it out by holding my head under a rivulet of rainwater running off the roof, letting it flow into my ear, but the bug held tight.

I did not know what to do. I shook my head from side to side and pounded on my skull above the affected ear, with no result. I attempted to sleep with that side of my head down, hoping that gravity might work its mysterious magic; however, gravity did not move my unwanted new passenger one iota. Isaac Newton failed me. I ended up tossing and turning without relief from the constant irritation. I even believed, from time to time, that I could hear a faint noise from the embedded bug. I dismissed the sound I heard, attributing it the storm, possibly static electricity from the highly charged air around me.

I lay in bed through the night, not sleeping a wink. When morning came, with the critter still lodged firmly in place, I paid a visit to the island's medicine man to see if he might remove it. By medicine man, I mean native witchdoctor. I had no faith that he would help, but I was desperate. He looked in my ear and even held a burning torch so close I could smell my hair burning but saw nothing. This "wise" man lacked the tools required for the task. My unwelcome voyager remained aboard.

On boarding my ship, I again tried flushing the creature from my ear with liberal doses of seawater. I even dove under water, for as long as I could hold my breath. My resident source of constant irritation remained. Relief would have to await San Francisco. The fear of what it might be doing was driving me mad. My futile efforts to relieve my anxiety delayed our sailing until the afternoon high tide, but we finally sailed away.

I suffered day after day. I repeated, without success, prior remedies, pouring salt water into my ear and pounding my palm into the side of my head in an attempt to dislodge it until my head hurt. My tormented mind and my sensations of the bug's occasional movement kept me from sound sleep.

Frustration from the constant sensation of having a foreign object so close to my brain and lack of sleep drove me nearly to madness during the voyage.

On arriving in San Francisco, after securing my illicit cargo, I rushed to the nearest physician for relief. My anticipation of relief grew with every stride towards the doctor's office.

I hastily explained my plight and torment. He pulled down his light reflector from his forehead, and retrieved a magnifying glass from a drawer, to enlarge his view into my ear canal. On inspection, he hemmed, and he hummed, and finally, he announced that he could see nothing. He said he saw no bug, no obstruction - not even an irritation.

Flabbergasted, I insisted that he was wrong - I could feel the bug's presence at that instant. I demanded that he look again, and the doctor humored me. He even touched along the walls of my ear canal close to my eardrum with a thin metal probe. Again, he found nothing - no bite, no movement, nothing revealing the presence of a living insect. I could tell he was beginning to think I was suffering from severe delusions. However, I was not imagining the sensations.

I exploded. I screamed. To calm, or more likely placate, me, the doctor suggested that the bug might be hiding in my eustachian tube. I yelled, "No, the bug is right here in my ear canal." The doctor refused to look again and merely suggested that I wait to see if the sensation subsided. I told him that weeks had gone by, and the irritation had not subsided in the slightest. Thinking perhaps that I was mad, he left me sitting and walked out.

Frustrated by his diagnosis, I saw two more doctors. The result was the same, no real answers. The third one had the nerve to suggest that I might be suffering a mental breakdown caused by my long voyage. He placated me by suggesting my delusion might be temporary - my only hope. Was I crazy? I believed in my heart that I was not.

I went about my business that day with my infernal irritation pulsing in and out of my consciousness throughout the day. I sent a messenger to advise my buyers of their appointed times and locations for meeting with me the following day.

As I had no permanent residence, I went to a hotel to sleep, exhausted from my weeks of fitful sleep. As I lay down, with sleep rapidly approaching, I felt the bug move. Then, to my surprise, I heard someone say, "Do not do it." I sprang from my bed and scanned every corner of my room. I saw no one. Then, I thought perhaps the voice had carried through the thin hotel walls; however, listening closely to each, I heard no sounds through either wall. I could have sworn that the statement had come from my room, if not even from within my ear. I began to consider that I had gone crazy. Not only could I feel the footsteps of an invisible bug moving in my ear; now, I was hearing it speak to me. I lay down once more to see if I would hear it again, but only silence ensued. My sleep that night was more restless than ever.

The next morning, my messenger returned to my hotel room and confirmed that my buyers were ready and would meet that evening at the times I specified. The first would be at six o'clock at the Jade Garden, a colorful but discreet restaurant in Chinatown. I sent the messenger away.

No sooner had I closed the door than I again heard from deep within my ear canal, "Do not do it." This time, being on my feet, alert and awake, no further doubt existed - I had heard what I thought I heard. The bug was talking to me.

I considered returning to the doctor or seeing another doctor but feared being committed to an asylum. If they saw and heard nothing again, and I told them that I heard the bug speak, they would order up a wagon - to haul me off as a danger to others. Then, I realized what the bug had said, and I unconsciously spoke aloud, "Why not?" To which, to my further shock and now growing fascination, I heard the bug reply, "Because I said so."

The bug spoke, in plain English, with no accent whatsoever, which belied its origin. How could a bug talk? How could a bug that talks speak English? Why would a bug care what I was up to? My head was spinning with questions. Either I was carrying on a conversation with a talking bug, or I had gone mad and was talking to myself. I was no longer sure.

With my head running in circles of irresolvable logic, I finally blurted out, "Why are you saying I should stop and who do you think you are to demand that I change?" To which the bug responded, "Because what you are doing is wrong, and because I know right from wrong, something you do not." For once, I was speechless. It sounded like somebody's conscience talking. However, I knew *my* conscience was not doing the talking, because I had forsaken mine years ago. I knew the voice had not arisen from my long-suppressed conscience, but I had no clue where it came from.

My head swam. I could not understand why the doctors did not see it, or him , I had concluded that the bug was male in gender because of its aggressiveness. I wondered what he possibly could do to me if I proceeded with my plan. I even considered asking him to tell me how to extract him from my ear. I settled for the last question and posed it to the bug, "How can I get you out of my ear?" In the same vein as before, the bug replied, "By doing what is right."

Confused, I asked, "If I forgo this business deal, are you saying that you will leave?" To which the bug replied, "No. My expectations reach beyond one deal. You must exchange your evil ways for good and do so forever."

Suddenly, I felt pain. The pain lasted longer than other quick, sharp pains I have experienced. The pain lasted for what seemed like hours but was only seconds. My eyes watered; my right hand went instinctively to cover my ear, and my mind went into flight. When the pain subsided and my mind reengaged, I asked, "Did you just bite me?" The bug answered, "Yes, and I will do so repeatedly unless you change your evil ways. If you do not, then I will carry on munching and, in less than three days, reach your brain and start eating it."

Completely befuddled, I blurted, "But I don't know any other way to earn a living – no honest ways." The bug replied, "You are smart; you can learn."

I retorted, "And if I sincerely try and fail?"

He replied, "You must not fail. I have a voracious appetite that is only controlled by eliminating evil, and I am plenty hungry."

I thought and thought. I must find a way out of this. I reasoned as follows: If I start doing good deeds, and he leaves, then I can return to my old ways. Perhaps I could even squash him as he leaves or, better yet, capture him and make money from exhibiting him around the world – "See the talking beetle!" I could envision operating a sideshow at fairs and carnivals. I chose to play along.

Before I could speak, another sharp, searing pain shot through my head, even worse than the first-time – a combination of pinch and burn but sharper and lasting longer – like biting your tongue. It took me minutes to recover this time instead of seconds.

The bug said, "Let me answer some of your questions. The doctors cannot see me because we bugs have developed over eons an amazing ability to blend into the world around us – what you might call camouflage; we call survival. I speak English because my relatives traveled with Captain Cook and taught me the language when I was young. They also taught me right from wrong. When I leave, you will not squash me because I am too quick. You asked who put me in charge. I did." That was when I grasped that, not only was the bug talking and listening to me, but it could also hear my thoughts. I was already crushed physically, and now I was crushed mentally. I did not know what to do, think, or say.

At this point, I had to face reality. I had to reevaluate my thinking, even my life, and consider what my remaining options were. I could fight against this determined bug and try to endure the escalating pain and injury, or I could give up my opium business and take on a new life. I could think of no other options, with my thinking befuddled from the pain. At this point, I was leaning heavily toward starting a new life as the only escape. As my thinking cleared on what I had to do, the bug said, "Now that you seem to understand, I will leave you tonight. However, do not forget. I will return if you revert to your evil ways."

I stepped out of my room to send a message through the hotel clerk to my messenger that the meetings scheduled for this evening were canceled. Then I returned to my room.

After the last declaration from the bug and my action in canceling the meeting, our conversation appeared to be ended. I lay down to sleep, exhausted but with a sense of lightness, as if a weight had been lifted off me. I finally slept at ease – a deep sleep - catching up for weeks of extraordinary strain.

On awakening, I felt immediately that the bug was gone. My sense of relief was inexpressible. To be free of the constant irritation, the fear of being bitten again, and the moral judgments about my behavior made me giddy. I jumped up and danced around the room, stopping every three or four hops to listen and feel - to convince myself that the bug was truly gone. Had I just awoken from a dream? Might I have been temporarily insane for a time? The memory of the searing pain was too fresh in my nerves to have been a dream, and I was not behaving crazily in any other regard.

Then, I began to think. The bug is gone. I could still complete my business transaction after all. I had not forgotten that I had promised to start a new life, but greed is a seductive temptress – muddling the mind and distorting rational thoughts.

I considered the possibilities. I had not forgotten the bug's threat to return. However, if I went ahead with the transaction, I needed a way to protect myself for when the bug returned, as I believed it would. Then, an innovative solution came to me. I would plug my ears with cotton whenever I lay down. That way, I could thwart the return of the bug. I sent a new message to my contacts, saying that the meetings were back on.

At the appointed time, I met my contact, transferred the opium, collected my money, and went back to my hotel. On my way back to the hotel, I stopped by an apothecary and purchased cotton balls.

That evening, delighted with my ingenuity and success, I celebrated by eating and drinking heavily. When it grew late, I retired to my room, plugged my ears with cotton, lay down, and fell again into a deep slumber. My sense of satisfaction was complete.

Then, in the midst of my deepest sleep, my consciousness suddenly became aware of tiny footsteps on my arm. I thought, hah! Wait until he gets to my ear this time. Won't he be shocked? I also decided that I had better squash him. He could still bite my arm or face. I began to move toward swatting the bug, when suddenly a terrible new sensation came over me.

I could feel another bug on my other arm and then one, no two, on my leg. Next, I felt more. Bugs were crawling over me, marching along my arms, legs, and torso. Swarms of them ran rapidly to every part of my body. I could feel thousands of tiny footsteps. My mind raced, trying to think of what to do, while fighting against panic. I wanted to run for the bathtub down the hall but was paralyzed by fear. Then, I heard, distinctly and clearly, a single word command from the first bug on my arm, "Now!"

At that instant, my entire body convulsed in pain. Hundreds, if not thousands, of bugs bit me simultaneously on every accessible body part. I was bitten from the bottom of my feet to the top of my head. My flesh burned, stung, and ripped. I could feel the bugs eating me alive - blood oozing from the bites. The pain cannot be described. My mind flooded with pain, to the exclusion of every other possible thought except the fear of every piece of flesh being stripped from my body. I screamed, "Okay. I promise. I will be forever good. Stop and I will change my ways and become the man you say I should be. I will give my ill-gotten gains to the poor and the orphans and others in need. Please stop!"

The biting ceased and the pain subsided marginally but remained intense and burning at a barely tolerable level. I could feel the bugs retreating except for the one on my arm. I felt him move up toward my ear. When he arrived at my ear, he stopped and whispered through my cotton plug, in a low but audible voice, "Your promise must not be like a casual plea to God in a moment of need, easily made but quickly forgotten. You can never break your promise again. Next time it will be fatal. And just so you know, I can chew through cotton in no time. And you have other orifices."

That is the truth of how I came to be covered in scars. They are not from war or misfortune, but from a reckoning. I will tell my fiancée only part of it, enough to explain the marks, not enough to haunt her dreams. I will say I was a smuggler once, and that my past caught up with me in the worst of ways. I will not mention the bug. Not unless he comes back. And I pray, with every honest breath I take, that he never does.

Boothbay Harbor, Maine -- April 1999

SUNDAY, APRIL 12

Most people wouldn't think an antique dealer in the quiet village of Boothbay Harbor, Maine, could make a comfortable living selling the flotsam and jetsam of dead ships, and the occasional dead seafarer. Nevertheless, I managed to do so. Nautical antiquities were my specialty. And like many who live near the sea, and even a few who don't, I often dreamt of finding a vast pirate treasure that would bring me fortune and fame.

My best friend, Jack Bartow, Boothbay's police chief and a local fixture, couldn't have cared less about pirate treasure, unless it had been stolen. My mother, bless her soul, only cared why Jack and I weren't married, engaged, or at least dating.

I was sitting on the corner of Jack's desk in the only room that comprised the town's police station. During the day, Jack, his two deputies, and his assistant worked out of the front room of his two-room building; at night, Jack lived in the back. The décor of the office reflected both his job and his outlook, an odd mix of commendations and old photos of shipwrecks, hurricane damage, a shark attack, and two drownings. When he first returned from eight years in the Army to take over as police chief, he told me he kept those photos as reminders: life could end suddenly, whether from Mother Nature or human nature.

As he finished his monthly crime report, I gazed through the station's windows at a gorgeous schooner gliding through the harbor and tucking neatly into its dock slip. She had the same quiet strength that reminded me of Jack.

He was six feet tall, almost a foot taller than me. We were both fit and in our mid-thirties, though Jack's dark hair was already thinning and streaked grey. While he'd been in the Army, I worked as an EMT for two years, then tried college in Boston. That didn't stick, but apprenticing in a Boston antique shop did. That's what eventually brought me back to Boothbay Harbor to open my own shop. Jack returned three years later.

His office sat like the tip of a spear where Oak and Todd Streets met, both lined with shops and pointed directly at the marina, the heart of the village. In the spring of 1999, Boothbay Harbor was everything you'd expect from a coastal Maine postcard: crisp sea-salt air, rocky coastlines, lobster fishermen, boatbuilders, and a constellation of islands once rumored to shelter pirate gold. I didn't know it then, perched as I was in Jack's office, but we were about to become treasure hunters or that Jack would soon have to revise his "meager monthly crime statistics" report to the state.

I was about to invite Jack to dinner; I'd had a profitable day selling a dozen brass portholes and a ship's compass to the Davy Jones' Locker seafood chain, when Bonnie Martin burst through the door.

"Chief, I need your help!" she hollered. "Bill's missing! He should've been back by noon, and I can't raise him on the radio."

Jack stood immediately and reached out to steady her. "Red, pull that chair over for Bonnie," he said. "When did you last see him?"

Everyone else called me Judy, but Jack had called me Red since we were kids sailing matching Sailfishes in the

140

harbor. My brunette hair turned a fiery red in the sun, and the name stuck. Bonnie's hair had once been vivid red, though it had faded to sandy gray. Her temper, however, hadn't faded in the slightest, she was known all over town for being hot-headed. But now she looked genuinely shaken, and I moved quickly. Jack guided her into the chair with one hand on her shoulder.

"He must've taken the boat out before dawn," she said. "We had a spat last night. He slept on the couch. I didn't even hear him leave. Didn't get to say goodbye."

"I know you're both strong-willed," Jack said gently. "But did things get abusive again?"

"No!" she exclaimed, her voice cracking as tears welled.

Still, something about her posture, tense, guarded, set off quiet alarms in my head. My intuition was picking up something unsaid.

"How early do you think he left?" Jack asked.

"About two a.m.," Bonnie said.

"Why so early?"

"He believed someone was poaching his traps," she said. "We were arguing, he'd gotten obsessive. I told him the catch was down for everyone, but he wouldn't listen. What if he was right? What if he caught someone in the act?"

"Let's not get ahead of ourselves," Jack said.

Bill Martin was a hard-working local lobsterman and the loudest voice in the Maine Lobstermen's Association. He constantly butted heads with the Department of Fisheries and picked fights with other lobstermen over quotas and regulations. His combative streak could easily be tied to his disappearance. While it wasn't unusual for a lobsterman to run

141

late, Bonnie not being able to reach him by radio sent an ominous ripple down my spine.

"We'll send the launch out first," Jack said. "Could be engine trouble, or maybe the radio went. If we don't find him soon, I'll call in the Coast Guard." I could see my dinner plans slipping away.

"Please let me know the second you hear anything," Bonnie said, as she walked out the door.

"Can we squeeze in a quick dinner while your deputies investigate?" I asked. "Something about her story isn't sitting right with me, and I'd like to talk it through."

"Might be seen as shirking my duty by a few folks," Jack said, "but Bill Martin's shining personality has won over so many that I doubt anyone will mind if I let Don and Randy handle it. Let's go."

"Can we squeeze in a quick dinner while your deputies investigate?" I asked. "Something about her story isn't sitting right with me, and I'd like to talk it through."

"Might be seen as shirking my duty by a few folks," Jack said, "but Bill Martin's shining personality has won over so many that I doubt anyone will mind if I let Don and Randy handle it. Let's go."

Don Hall, Jack's senior deputy, was in his late twenties, six-foot-two, strong, and weatherworn handsome. He was from Boston and rarely pronounced his r's. Randy Clark, the junior deputy, was barely twenty-two, wiry, redheaded, freckled, and fresh on the job. He came from Mississippi, and though he'd lived in Chicago for a few years, he still carried a soft, charming drawl. Both had served in the Army, though not during Jack's time.

At that moment, Don and Randy were out on the harbor in the police launch, replacing a lamp on a buoy near the harbor entrance. Jack and I reached the marina just as they were pulling the launch back up to the dock. Jack waved them over and redirected them to head back out, this time to look for Bill Martin's boat. Don knew the local lobster zones like his own backyard; he'd know where to begin the search.

"They'll be out at least an hour or two," Jack said as we watched them head back out. "How about the Chowder House? Could be a long night."

Back at the station, before we left, Jack called Josie Fleur, his part-time assistant, and asked her to come in and monitor the radio in case Don or Randy checked in, or in the unlikely event another crime interrupted our quiet little harbor. Josie lived just a block away, so we didn't wait for her to arrive. Being Boothbay Harbor, Jack didn't even bother locking the front door.

As we reached the Chowder House, we passed my mother on her way out.

"Hello, Mrs. Johnson," Jack said, tipping his hat with that old-school charm my mother adored.

"Oh, how lovely to see you two out together," she beamed.

"Not too subtle," I muttered under my breath.

The Chowder House always felt like home with red checkered tablecloths, home-cooked food, and fishing lures dangling from netting strung above the booths. We ate in near silence. Jack ordered pork chops; I went for the lobster fra diavolo. I could eat lobster every day, but Jack had hit his lifetime quota sometime around 1974.

"So, Red, what's your intuition telling you?" he asked, finally setting down his fork.

"It's not entirely clear. But I sense Bonnie knows more than she's telling us."

"Us? You joined my police force while I wasn't looking?"

"You know you need a woman's intuition on any major case," I said. "You need me." Jack rolled his eyes. "Well, this isn't a major investigation."

As if to prove my point, in walked the harbormaster.

Willy Parker was a gruff, gray-haired, gray-bearded bear of a man in overalls. He ran the marina with an iron fist attitude.

Don't like havin' to chase all over, lookin' for ya," he grumbled. "Why ain't ya in your office where you're s'posed to be?" Jimmy's dead.

"Your assistant, Jimmy Farrow?" I asked.

"Who else 'round here's named Jimmy?" he said. "He's layin' there at the end o' the east-most dock."

"Can you tell us what happened?" Jack asked, as we both rose to follow Willy.

"No idea," Willy said.

I whispered to Jack, "Well, now we have a major investigation."

"We'll be there in a second," Jack said. "Don't touch a thing."

"I ain't stupid," Willy said as he walked out.

As Jack quickly paid the bill and we moved toward the exit, Josie rushed in.

"Don's on the radio, needs to talk to you."

Jack jogged back to his office, and I followed, six feet behind. He sprang through the open door and grabbed the radio microphone. It crackled to life.

"Go ahead," Jack said.

"We're in a small cove along the west coast of Damariscove Island," Don said. "We found Martin's boat, the *Marianne*. She's sunk but bow up, we can see her name."

"Any sign of a body? Any sign of violence?" Jack asked.

"No signs of eitha' yet."

"Any chance he swam ashore?"

"Not likely heah. The shoah bouldahs are big and steep."

We both knew the water was still brutally cold. A man wouldn't last more than a few minutes, certainly not long enough to swim to shore through icy surf.

"Call Stillman Salvage over at New Harbor," Jack said. "Have them come raise the boat. Bring lights. By the time they get there, visibility will be black as tar, no full moon tonight. Also, call for Coast Guard divers to search for the body. Call me when, or should I say if, you find it."

"Will do," Don said.

Josie had followed us back to the station, still looking flustered.

"Josie, monitor the phones," Jack said. "I'll be at the marina. And call the coroner, we've got a body to retrieve down there."

"Whose?" she asked.

"Jimmy Farrow," Jack replied.

"Oh dear," she whispered.

Jack headed out the door toward the docks. I followed, just a step behind.

"Since my deputies are tied up," he said, glancing over his shoulder and noticing me on his heels, "you might as well come along as a witness while I check out how Jimmy died. You're not squeamish, are you?"

"If you remembered important little details about me," I said, "you'd know I was an EMT for two years after high school."

Sunday Evening June 12

The sun had slipped below the horizon in the few minutes it took us to reach the dock where Jimmy lay, not far from a gleaming sixty-foot Viking Sport Fisher. I knew a boat like that cost well over a million dollars. I often dreamed of owning one someday.

The harbormaster, the gruff Mr. Parker, scurried about the dock, switching on lights as darkness settled in. On the weathered planks, Jimmy Farrow's body lay spread-eagle. His usual brightness, lilting Irish accent, and those boyish freckles had faded into the ashen stillness of death.

One outstretched hand pointed seaward with a stiffened forefinger. A single bullet hole pierced the center of his chest.

Powder burns marked his shirt, so he had been shot at close range. Blood had pooled around him and seeped between the planks into the water. It had already dried into a dark, rust-colored smear. His eyes stared upward until I knelt and gently closed them.

Jack unbuttoned Jimmy's shirt to inspect the wound.

"A .38 caliber would be my educated guess," he said.

"Could be a nine millimeter," I replied. "How long do you think he's been dead?"

Jack gave me one of those looks, the kind that reminded me the difference between those calibers was less than a tenth of a millimeter.

"Hard to say without checking body temp. I'm guessing last night. Willy, why didn't you spot the body during the day?"

"None of the big boats at the seaward end moved today," Willy said. "They block my view from the shack porch."

"You didn't miss him?"

"Today was his day off," Willy said.

Jack stepped aboard the Sport Fisher and checked its log.

He jumped back onto the dock. "No entries for over a week."

Suddenly, I stopped cold. Off the stern of the Sport Fisher, right where Jimmy's rigid finger had been pointing, something bobbed in the water.

Jack caught me staring. "What is it?"

"What's that lobster trap doing in the marina?" I asked.

"Somebody might be living aboard and trying to catch dinner," Jack said. "Wait."

"Exactly," I cut in. "That buoy has Bill Martin's red, gray, and yellow striping. That pot is way out of bounds."

Jack grabbed a boat hook from a nearby post, snared the rope beneath the buoy, and hauled it toward the dock. Usually, lobstermen used powered winches to bring in traps. The job wasn't easy, even for Jack, who was as strong as a bull. The trap was soaked, heavy, encrusted in seaweed, and filled with more than lobsters.

147

He finally hauled it up and dropped it onto the planks with a thud. I jumped back as seawater splashed across my shoes.

Jack flipped the slatted latch and opened the trap's door. A sodden burlap sack was inside, nestled between the netting and a few startled lobsters.

It wasn't full, but it looked heavy.

Jack pulled it out, water streaming from its coarse weaving, and unknotted the top. I leaned over his shoulder as he reached in and drew out a golden goblet inlaid with emeralds the size of marbles.

"Holy cow," I breathed, taking it gently from his hands. "This is incredible. Pre-Columbian, maybe."

"Is it solid gold?" Jack asked.

"Much more than that," I said, examining the workmanship. "What else is in the sack?"

Jack reached in and pulled out a handful of the contents.

"Coins," he said.

"Gold doubloons and silver reales," I added, inspecting them without letting go of the goblet. "These are marvelous. But this goblet... it's incredible. It's worth a fortune. A big one. Anything else besides coins?"

"Nope," Jack said. "This could be part of a bigger find."

"That's likely," I said. "We need to find the rest of the treasure before it disappears into the underground market."

"Well, this stash must be the motive for Jimmy's murder," Jack said.

"And whoever killed him had to be a stranger. Any local would've recognized Martin's buoy as out of place and figured out where Jimmy hid the loot. I guess dead men do tell tales."

"It also might mean the killer's still around," Jack said. "Because he hasn't found this sack yet. I need to talk to Willy again."

"You said 'he,'" I pointed out. "Couldn't the killer have been a woman?"

"Not likely," Jack said. "Guns are rarely a woman's M.O."

I gently placed the goblet back into the sack to keep it safe.

Jack took the bag from me as we walked toward Willy Parker, who was rocking lazily on his porch like none of the night's chaos mattered. When we reached him, I turned and looked back. Jimmy's body wasn't visible from this vantage point. Willy eyed the burlap sack but didn't ask.

"I only recall hearing two boats after I went to bed," he said.

Willy lived aboard a twenty-seven-foot, 1961 fiberglass Tartan sloop in front of his shack. He only took it out once or twice a summer.

"Do you know which boats they were?" I asked.

"The one that went out around 10:00 p.m. had a throaty diesel sound. It could've been that big Sport Fisher. The other went out well after midnight. I'd say sometime between one and four a.m. Had the slow putt-putt rhythm of a lobsterman."

"You only heard them?" I asked. "You didn't actually see the boats?"

"Had no reason to crawl outta bed at that hour," Willy snapped.

Just then, I spotted the coroner's van approaching. I nudged Jack.

149

We returned to Jimmy's body and waited while it was formally removed.

Later, we carried the treasure to my antique shop, where an old bank safe stood in the corner like a sleeping iron beast, black, squat, mounted on rusted wheels. It had come with the building years ago. I'd tracked down the manufacturer to reset the combination and service the locking mechanism. It opened as smoothly as silk.

I carefully placed the goblet on the bottom shelf, the only one tall enough to accommodate its height. Jack counted the coins and logged each for the custody receipt I needed to sign.

"This pile of gold and silver, including that goblet, gives us plenty of motive for murder," I said, flipping through an old auction catalog of maritime treasures. "But we don't have any suspects."

Jack nodded grimly. "The other thing we don't know yet is whether Bill Martin's disappearance, the damage to his boat, and Jimmy's murder are all connected or just pieces of a much bigger puzzle."

"I'll call a Boston friend of mine and see if he'll come up and help us learn more about this treasure," I said.

Jack returned to the station to open a file on the murder case, and I headed home.

My mother, Judith—yes, I was named after her—lived with me in my cottage just northwest of my shop, half a block from the police station. The house was a New England cliché: a white bungalow with blue trim, a whitewashed picket fence, and an interior decorated in nautical colors, lots of light blue and white, with paintings of three-masted schooners and maritime antiques tucked into nearly every corner.

When I walked through the door, Mother looked up from her needlepoint.

"Jimmy Farrow's dead," I told her. "Shot."

She gasped and pressed her hand to her chest. I didn't mention the treasure, not because I didn't trust her, but because she was a bit of a gossip.

"When will Jack be asking you to marry him?" she asked.

"We're not even dating," I said. "Why would he propose when we don't even have a romantic relationship?"

"You should start one," she said pointedly. "And what are you waiting for? You'll be a spinster before much longer."

"Ouch," I mumbled.

I dropped the subject. I knew better. If I'd dared mention that I wanted financial independence before marriage, it would've triggered a sermon about "letting a man take care of me." I didn't want a relationship built on dependence.

MIDDAY, MONDAY, APRIL 13

Just before noon the next day, Rodney Trowbridge strolled into my shop. The place was a haven for lovers of the sea: old maps in frames, navigating instruments, half-hull ship models, and a rare sea captain's desk I'd recently acquired. Rodney stood six-foot-two, thin and composed, with auburn hair, and always dressed like a man trying to impress someone. Today: dark grey suit, crisp white shirt, no tie. As he stepped inside, he casually glanced around, assessing whether anything on display was worthy of his appraiser's regard.

He didn't comment, so apparently, nothing was.

151

"Greetings, Lady Judith!" Rodney announced in his mild English accent.

I looked up from one of my reference books and gave a theatrical start.

"Hello, Rodney, you old British fox," I said, rising from my stool. I jogged around the counter and gave him a big hug. Brits get squirmy about affection, and I loved tweaking his primness. I'd known Rodney for over a decade and often relied on his sharp appraiser's eye.

"Are you well?" I asked, looking up into his now-blushing face.

"Bully, as Teddy Roosevelt would say," he replied. "You said you had something worth my attention?"

"What treasures have you been seeing lately?" I asked.

"Nothing inspiring," he said. "Seems like all the best pieces were long ago discovered and locked away in museums or the vaults of the ultra-wealthy."

"Well," I said, walking over to the safe, "let me show you something that might reignite your passion for maritime history."

I opened the safe, removed the gleaming goblet, and placed it gently in front of him.

"Blimey," he breathed. "This is... awe-inspiring." He picked it up delicately, turned it slowly, and then set it down with the care of a man handling a relic from a sacred altar. "I should be wearing white gloves."

"How old do you think it is?" I asked, placing a few of the gold coins beside it.

"My initial estimate is early fourteenth century," he said. "Spanish, possibly looted from Colombia. It might've made its way to Portugal or directly to Spanish nobility. But the design is ringing bells. I've seen something like this before, though I can't place it. Let me sketch it. I'll take the drawing back with me and check my references."

I handed Rodney a tape measure, paper, and pencil, and he began to draw with the kind of precision that came naturally to him.

"I've got a Polaroid camera if you'd prefer," I offered.

"A drawing picks up more detail," he said. "And I can annotate what I draw."

I watched him measure and sketch. His freehand skills were impressive.

"Think there might be an opportunity for me to broker the sale of these pieces, assuming the rightful owner can't be found?" I asked.

"Not for a long time," Rodney said. "The state's antiquities act will come into play. They'll want to examine each piece, determine provenance, and investigate whether a claim still exists. And if someone found these and didn't report it promptly? That could be a felony."

"A felony? Even if they turned it in?"

"If they waited more than five business days to notify authorities. There could even be an old insurance policy floating around."

"An insurance company? From the 1600s?"

"Lloyds of London started in 1741," Rodney said. "If the ship was insured through them, or if later pieces were, there might be legal entanglements. It'll take years to establish clear title."

"Drat," I muttered. "That'll take more patience than suits me."

When he finished the drawing, Rodney promised to call in a day or two. I returned the goblet to the safe, locked up, and headed toward Jack's office.

But before I reached it, I saw the police launch guiding in Stillman's tugboat, which towed a large, flat salvage barge. Bill Martin's lobster boat was sitting atop it at a listing angle.

Jack emerged from the station just as I reached the street. We fell into step together, heading for the marina.

Stillman's barge pulled up to the main dock. The tide was out, so the walkway aligned perfectly with the gunwale. Bernard Stillman stepped ashore first.

He was in his mid-fifties, barrel-chested and thick-limbed but softening around the middle. Everyone in town knew his story: once a tough salvage man, now a power-hungry businessman and loud voice on the town council. His thinning hair, bloated pride, and well-fed ambition marked a man still clawing for more.

Two muscular crewmen followed him, hauling gear and looking grim.

The barge had lifted the *Marianne* onto its flat deck using an onboard crane, an effective way to preserve any potential evidence.

"Looks like a shotgun blast through the hull," Stillman said, chewing a toothpick.

"Any sign of Bill Martin?" Jack asked just as Don stepped off the police launch.

"None so far," Don replied. "The Coast Guard is on scene, searching with divers. No shotgun either."

"I'll tally up time and fuel and send you the bill," Stillman added as he strolled toward his wife, Molly, who waited beside her gleaming black Mercedes. She looked like a magazine model, bleached-blonde, designer sunglasses, and most likely entirely devoted to her husband's credit line.

Jack and I climbed onto the barge and circled the *Marianne* like buzzards. The hole in the hull sat just below the waterline, formed by two nearly parallel blasts from a shotgun.

"Not accidental," I said. "Double-barreled shotguns don't usually fire both barrels at once."

"Unless modified," Jack added. "Either way, someone had to drop into or lean into the engine compartment to fire upward from inside."

"Bill wouldn't sink his boat," I said as we stepped off the barge and onto the walkway.

"I'll update Bonnie Martin," Jack said.

"I'll do an informal canvas of the shop owners, see if anyone heard or saw anything suspicious around the harbor two nights ago."

"Keep it informal," Jack said. "Remember, you're not deputized. If you hear anything remotely connected to this case, pass it on to Don or me. We need it legally admissible."

Jack didn't expect the canvas to turn up anything useful. Otherwise, he wouldn't have let me handle it solo. He figured anything that happened in the middle of the night wasn't likely to have been witnessed by shop owners already home in bed. But I just thought feeding my intuition couldn't hurt.

Before starting my rounds, I stopped by my shop to check phone messages and collect the mail that had dropped through the slot. While inside, the phone rang.

"Where have you been?" my mother asked. "I called your shop and then Jack's office. You weren't at either. I wanted to know what you'd like for dinner."

"Mother, I'm a grown woman. I could be anywhere. In this case, I was at the marina. Bill Martin's boat was found sunk in a cove off Damariscove. He's missing."

"Doesn't surprise me," she said. "Most people couldn't stand that hothead."

"Don't wait dinner for me," I said.

I headed up the south side of the street, speaking with each shopkeeper. No leads. Circling back down the north side, I paused before entering Louie Vintner's place. I was reluctant to deal with the scourge of the local nautical antique business.

Vintner was everything I despised in the trade: a shady dealer who passed off reproductions as originals, peeled "Made in China" labels from cheap knockoffs, and priced them like genuine artifacts. He had no shame. But for the greater good, and Jack, I squared my shoulders and walked into the lion's den.

Vintner looked up from a ledger, startled. "What do you want?" he snapped, quickly slamming the book shut. A police scanner buzzed on the counter behind him. He reached over and turned it down.

"Jack Bartow asked me to canvas the shop owners," I said, stretching the truth slightly. "Seen or heard anything strange around the harbor in the last forty-eight hours?"

From where he sat, Vintner had a near-perfect view of the harbor.

"I've noticed plenty of activity around the dock the last couple of days, but I've been too busy to investigate," he said. "What's been happening?"

"For one, Jimmy Farrow was murdered, shot in the chest the night before last," I said. "And Bill Martin has disappeared. His boat was sunk by a shotgun blast through the hull."

I thought I caught the briefest flicker of surprise cross Vintner's face, but it vanished as quickly as it came.

"I saw no one and heard nothing that would bear on either event," he said. "Although I am sorry to hear about Jimmy."

"On another topic, have you seen or heard of any recent treasure finds?" I asked. "Anyone try to sell you antique treasure in the last couple of days?"

Again, I saw something, maybe a blink, a hesitation.

"What type of treasure?" he asked.

I felt he was deliberately coy, though maybe my bias clouded my reading.

"Any type," I replied, matching his ambiguity.

"No," he said, smiling thinly. "But surely you'll let me know if any is to be found hereabouts."

"I will if you'll do likewise," I said, opening the door and stepping outside.

I walked past Vintner's storefront, stopped, and waited thirty seconds before slowly leaning back to peek through the window.

He'd already returned to his desk and was frantically dialing the phone. I couldn't hear him or see who he was calling, but I could see he was agitated, waving his free hand as he spoke.

That alone was worth reporting.

On the way back to Jack's office, I ran into my mother, who was coming from the opposite direction.

"What have you been up to?" I asked, narrowing my eyes.

"Oh, I just dropped by Jack's office," she said breezily.

"And why did you do that?"

"Just being neighborly," she replied with syrupy innocence.

"I'll talk to you this evening," I said, continuing toward the station.

When I arrived, Jack was back from visiting Bonnie Martin. He sat at his desk, thumbing through a glossy catalog filled with police gear, batons, tasers, duty belts, and high-powered flashlights.

"He's fascinated by new-fangled law enforcement gadgets," Josie whispered, shaking her head.

"Hey, thanks for the apple pie," Jack said, glancing up with a grin.

"You're thanking me for a pie?" I asked.

"Of course," he said. "Your mother told me how you made it for me last night."

"The shortest way to a man's heart is through his stomach," I mumbled.

"What was that?"

"Oh, I said you're welcome," I said. "How did your visit with Bonnie go?"

"I told her we had no word yet," Jack said. "And that we recovered his boat."

"Did you tell her about the hole in the hull?" I asked.

"Yes. Even though I doubted that Bill was still alive, I tried to sound optimistic. She shares those doubts."

"Did you ask if he carried a shotgun on board?"

"She said he did, but most lobstermen do. They worry about poachers," Jack said. "In years past, they'd use lighter loads and swap buckshot for rock salt."

"With the catch down like it is, I doubt they're so forgiving," I said.

"I also asked why he didn't report the poaching to me. Bonnie said he was stubborn and senselessly independent."

"No surprise there."

Just then, Don and Randy walked into the office.

"Any progress on Jimmy's death yet?" Jack asked.

Both deputies shook their heads.

"Vintner jumped on his phone before I was even out the door," I said. "He could be involved somehow."

"Based on what?"

"Intuition?"

"We can't request a search warrant for his phone records based on intuition," Jack said. "Well, we have no clues, but we can't just sit around waiting for one to fall in our laps. Don, take Randy at first light and head back to Damariscove Island. Do a thorough search, see if somehow Bill Martin made it ashore."

"I can't imagine he did but of course, we'll do it," Don said.

159

After the two deputies left, Jack and I tried to discuss the case for over an hour, but there wasn't much left to say. We were nowhere.

Finally, we retreated to our respective homes, Jack to his back room in just seconds, and me, living so close to my house, in minutes.

Mother was waiting up for me as if I were still in high school.

"I saved you some dinner in the oven if you're hungry," she said.

"Thanks, but I'm dieting," I said, lying, and went straight to bed, resisting the urge to call her out on her pie story or fuel her neighborhood rumor mill.

MORNING, TUESDAY, APRIL 14

The next morning, I was jolted awake at 7:00 by the jangle of the telephone beside my bed.

It was Rodney.

"I found it," he said.

"Found what?" I asked, still groggy.

"I knew something was familiar with that goblet," he said.

"What?"

"Huh?" I blinked. Then it hit me.

"The pirate?" I asked.

"Yes," Rodney replied. "But that's not the best part. Williams stole the goblet from another pirate, Edward English, down in the Bahamas and brought it north along with a vast accumulation of other loot."

"The Boston Maritime Museum has English's ship's log," he continued. "In it, he recorded the treasure, described the theft, and even sketched the goblet. The drawing looks exactly like the one I just did."

"So someone found treasure buried by Paulsgrave Williams, some of which he stole from another pirate," I said. "I have to tell Jack right away. That confirms his hunch that there's more treasure. And it strengthens the motive for murder."

"Murder?" Rodney asked sharply.

"I'll fill you in later. Gotta go. Thanks!" I hung up the phone.

I dressed quickly and stopped in the kitchen long enough to grab a piece of toast.

"Why don't you let me cook you a decent breakfast?" Mother asked.

"No time," I said. "Have to meet Jack."

"Oh, that's lovely," she called after me, thick with molasses.

I jogged out the door, wolfing toast, and headed straight down the street to Jack's office. As I arrived, we nearly collided, he came bursting out.

"We have to head to Damariscove Island," Jack said. "The boys found Bill Martin's body."

We ran to Jack's boat, a gleaming white 1960 twenty-two-foot downeast skiff with elegant lines and a graceful glide under his practiced hand. The sea was calm, the air warm and salty-sweet, and the sky a flawless bowl of blue. Ahead, a chain of small islands rose like green jewels, the village's gateway to the open ocean. The day's beauty stood in stark contrast to the grim task ahead.

Damariscove Island lies five nautical miles offshore. Once home to a small fishing community, now it was a refuge for the Common Eider, a rare seabird. Its tiny harbor offered modest shelter, and on the southern tip sat the crumbling remains of an old Coast Guard Life Saving Station.

We spotted the police launch moored at the island's only rickety dock and pulled alongside. Don met us at the head of the pier.

"This way," he said. "He's in that small grove of pines. We found a patch of disturbed earth, dug down, and uncovered his body."

The grave was too shallow to be proper. Bill lay face-up, legs sharply bent at the knees, partially covered in loose dirt. Randy brushed the soil from his face.

"Looks like the same caliber bullet," Jack said, noting the neat hole in Bill's forehead. "Lift him out."

Randy and Don carefully pulled the body from the hole and laid it beside the shallow grave.

Something glinted in the dirt below. I dropped into the hole and picked it up carefully by the edges.

"It's a gold coin," I said. "It looks just like the others."

"Others?" Don asked, helping me climb out.

"Yes. I haven't had the chance to tell you, we recovered a sack of gold and silver coins and a jeweled goblet from one of Bill's lobster traps in the harbor next to where Jimmy's body was found," Jack said. "Sorry, I didn't get to fill you in."

"Wow," Randy said. "Who does it belong to?"

"How did one of Bill's traps end up in the marina?" Don asked.

"It's all unclear at the moment," I said. "But for the record, I saw the buoy first."

"It's evidence," Jack said firmly. "And its ownership may not be clear for a long time. From the size and shape of this hole, I'd say a huge chest was removed. This discovery strengthens our belief that the treasure is much larger than what's currently in your safe."

"Well, at least two men had to be involved," I said.

"Because it would've taken two to carry the chest?" Randy asked.

"While that's probably true," Jack said, "she likely meant someone had to drive Bill's boat to where it was sunk."

"One would've followed in the treasure hunters' boat to pick up the second guy from the scuttled one," I added.

"Odds are high the same men killed Jimmy," Jack said.

"How do you figure?" Randy asked.

"Because we just don't have killers around here, and the murder weapon appears to be of the same caliber," Jack replied.

"And let's not forget the killers weren't locals," I said. "Otherwise, they'd have recognized Bill Martin's buoy on that trap next to where Jimmy was found."

"I still wonder how that trap ended up there," Randy said.

"Well, it's time I let Bonnie know about her husband," Jack said. "Don, you and Randy bring the body back to the harbor. The coroner can examine it on the police launch. No sense hauling him out here to confirm the obvious."

163

We speculated how it might've gone down as we walked to Jack's boat.

"Bill must have thought the treasure hunters were raiding his pots," I said. "He found them on the island and confronted them with his shotgun. Fearing he'd expose them, they shot him, buried the body, then used his own gun to scuttle the boat."

"That makes sense, mostly," Jack said. "But where does Jimmy fit in?"

"What if he was piloting their boat?" I offered. "Maybe he got greedy and stashed a few pieces for himself, hid them in that trap when they got back to the harbor."

"That's a theory," Jack said. "And it almost fits. Maybe they realized the goblet was missing?"

"Possibly. We don't know what else they found. They might've killed him just for skimming."

"Or because he witnessed what they uncovered," Jack added.

"Or even Bill's murder," I said. "Or they wanted a bigger share."

"There are plenty of motives," Jack said. "And just as many theories. But we still don't have a single suspect."

We reached Jack's skiff and headed back toward the harbor. The water shimmered under the rising sun, the kind of morning that usually promised peace, not bodies and buried treasure.

As we skimmed across the bay, I decided to test the waters another way.

"Jack," I said, "why have you never asked me out? I mean, on a real date?"

He was quiet a beat too long.

"I've thought about it," he said finally. "But since the last woman in my life died five years ago, I guess I've just gotten... comfortable."

"Stuck in your ways, huh?" I said, giving him a sidelong glance.

"We're different as people."

"How so?"

"You've always seemed to want a different kind of life than I do," Jack said. "Maybe bigger dreams, a faster pace. I'm more of a steady-as-she-goes guy."

"You wouldn't like those things?"

"I might like them. But I don't need them."

"Don't you want financial independence? The kind of security that comes with it?"

"I'm secure in my job, and that provides for my needs," Jack said. "But you've always struck me as someone who's aiming higher, for freedom, maybe, or to prove something. That's not a bad thing. It's just different."

His words didn't sting, exactly, but they surprised me. Did I really come across as someone chasing more just for the sake of it?

I looked out over the water and took a breath. "I don't want 'more' to impress anyone," I said. "I just want to build a life that's mine. That I earned."

Jack was quiet for a moment, then nodded. "That makes a lot more sense."

"A hunger for understanding. For something more lasting than gold," I said.

I looked out over the water and felt a chill that had nothing to do with the breeze.

165

If that's how he saw me, maybe there would never be more between us than friendship.

I resigned myself to that, for now.

LATER THAT DAY

We weren't back at the office long before the police launch motored into the harbor, and the coroner arrived by car to meet it. He boarded immediately while Don and Randy returned to the office to debrief.

"We dug down further in the hole and scoured the surrounding woods to see if we could spot depressions or other likely spots for additional treasure," Don said. "But we didn't find anything else promising."

"We're still waiting for our first real break," Jack said. "Don, take Randy and check every cabin rental, bed and breakfast, and motel in the county. See if two or more men checked in during the past few days. And be careful."

"Why don't I just call around?" Josie asked.

"Yes," Jack said patiently, "you could but you can't read the reaction on the desk clerk's face over the phone. We often tell when someone's lying by how they move or avoid eye contact."

Don glanced at Randy as if silently questioning whether his young partner had developed that particular talent yet. Jack saw it.

"You'll do fine. Just get moving," he said, waving them off with a flick of impatience.

"I'll take this coin to my shop and lock it up," I said. "Add one more to the log you started."

"I'll break the news to Bonnie," Jack said, updating his log sheet with practiced efficiency.

Afternoon, Tuesday, April 14

That afternoon, I returned to Jack's office just as Don and Randy came barreling in like a pair of mustangs.

"Tell me you've got a lead that'll crack this thing wide open," Jack said.

"We ended up with the strangest result surveyin' motels," Randy said.

"When we arrived at the Br'er Rabbit Motel," Don began.

"Where?" I asked.

"Br'er Rabbit Motel," Jack said. "The one out by the highway."

"Anyway, two guys checked out yesterday after a three-day stay," Don said.

"They paid cash and used fake names," Randy added. "Smith and Jones."

"Tell me the motel had video surveillance," Jack said, already frowning.

"Nope," Randy said. "They've got those fake cameras, just for show."

"So, what was strange?" I asked.

"The desk clerk said the two guys looked tough," Don said, gaining momentum. "The leader was about six feet tall. The other was maybe six inches shorter."

"They both had Southern accents," Randy added.

Jack looked thoughtful. "That fits the idea that they weren't local. Fake names, cash payment, Southern drawl, clearly trying not to be remembered."

"Did you get a vehicle description?" I asked.

"They arrived by taxi, according to the clerk," Don said. "Said they carried two duffels and a hard-sided case, like something a musician might use."

"Interesting, but still not particularly strange," Jack said.

"They left in a red Toyota pickup," Randy added.

"Did the clerk seem credible?" I asked.

"Hard to say," Don said. "Maybe."

"Did you check the room? The trash cans?" I asked.

"That's the strange part," Don said. "We did. And we found a business card from Mr. Vintner. It had fallen between the bed and the nightstand."

"See? I told you he was involved," I said.

"I wonder how he's connected to those two," Jack said, rubbing his temple.

"Did you check the 7-Eleven across from the motel?" I asked. "If they stopped in for coffee or snacks, their faces might've been caught on the store's security cameras."

"We didn't think of that," Don said. "We'll head there now."

He and Randy rushed out of the office.

Once they were gone, Jack said, "Now you're giving my men orders. Next thing you know, you'll be wantin' my job."

"Doesn't pay enough, Jack," I said. "Besides, I just confirmed, with absolute certainty, that the coin we found on the island matches the others. A tiny flaw across the reverse side, where the original stamping die must've had a hairline crack, proves it came from the same batch as the goblet and the other coins. It's all Paulsgrave Williams's treasure. Immensely valuable piece by piece, priceless if kept together and shown to the public, like the Crown Jewels."

Jack nodded thoughtfully. "Let's go talk to Willy Parker again. His lack of emotion over Jimmy's death has been eating at me."

We walked down to Willy's shack, where he was once again perched on his porch rocker.

"Hello again," he said. "What brings you back to my humble porch?"

"I've got a few more questions," Jack said.

"Fire away."

"Just to confirm, you said you were sleeping when Jimmy was killed, right?" Jack asked.

"Well, I probably was," Willy said. "I don't know exactly when he was killed."

"Very early morning," Jack said. "Possibly between four and five a.m."

"Then, yes, I would've been asleep."

"Did you hear a gunshot?" I asked.

"Nope," Willy replied. "Didn't hear a thing. But I'm a deep sleeper. I didn't wake up till about 7:15."

Jack gave him a long look. "I was also wondering about your reaction to Jimmy's death. You didn't seem all that affected."

"I saw worse in the war," Willy said. "That hardened me. If you're thinkin' I'm a suspect, let me save you the trouble. After I got outta the service, I vowed never to kill another livin' thing. I'm even a vegetarian."

"All right, then," Jack said with a nod. "Thanks."

As we walked back toward the office, Jack looked puzzled.

"What's on your mind?" I asked.

"He sounds believable," Jack said, "but something about his answers still doesn't sit right with me."

"The shooter must've used a silencer," I said. "Unusual for a small-town murder. That's more of a gangland move."

"Silencer's the only explanation, unless Willy sleeps like the dead," Jack said. "Or maybe he heard it and mistook it for a dream… or a flashback."

We arrived at the station just in time to hear Randy over the radio.

"Bad news, the 7-Eleven video wasn't working," he said. "Good news is we got a strong memory and a credit card."

"That's two things," Jack said dryly.

Don took the mic.

"The clerk didn't remember the men," he said, "but she retrieved a charge slip. They bought cigarettes with a credit card. The name on it was Jeanine Johnson."

"Give me a second," Josie said. She typed rapidly at her terminal.

"There," she said, pointing to the screen. "Jeanine Johnson. Lives at 781 East County Line Road."

"Don, drive to 781 East County Line," Jack said. "Proceed cautiously. Call for backup before going in if you see a red Toyota pickup."

"Will do," Don replied, signing off.

Jack turned to me. "Time to visit Louie Vintner. I want to know why two men at the Br'er Rabbit Motel had his business card."

"I've been waiting for this," I said.

"Stay calm," Jack warned. "Let me do the talking."

On the way up the street to Vintner's shop, we passed my mother heading who-knows-where. She gave us a wide grin as we walked by.

As we approached the storefront, we spotted Vintner behind his desk, watching us approach like a cat tracking a sparrow on a low branch.

When we walked in, Jack put on his small-town police chief charm.

"Hey, Louie," Jack called. "How's business?"

"Slower than yours seems to be," Vintner replied, shooting me a suspicious glance.

While they talked, I drifted around the shop, casually scanning the shelves for anything mispriced, just in case Vintner had slipped up and I could flip a profit.

"I'm sure you've heard what's going on," Jack said. "Anything you can tell us that might help the investigation?"

"What would I know?" Vintner said.

"One of my deputies found your business card in a motel room occupied by two suspicious individuals," Jack said. "Know anything about them?"

Vintner blinked, caught off guard, but recovered quickly.

"People come into my shop every day," he said. "I don't remember anyone I'd call 'rough.' Got a description?"

"One was about six feet tall, the other around five-foot-six," Jack said. "Both had an accent, possibly Southern. That's all we know until my deputies report back."

"I don't recognize anyone just from that description," Vintner replied.

"Okay," Jack said as we exited. "Call me if anything comes to mind later."

On the walk back to Jack's office, I could read the frustration in his jaw set.

"That wasn't particularly helpful," I said.

"He was evasive," Jack replied. "Still, we're nowhere. We need a break in this case."

We weren't back in the office long before Don came through on the radio again.

"The woman, Jeanine Johnson, claimed she didn't know her credit card was missing until we asked about it," Don said.

"Did she seem surprised?" Jack asked.

"Not really," Don said. "More annoyed than shocked. Like she's dealt with the police before. The motel clerk said she was at the Crossroads Saloon about a week ago, and that two strangers were hovering around her table. Probably lifted the card then."

"Another dead end," Jack muttered.

"Well, maybe not," Don said. "Here's the strange part, Jeanine described the men completely differently from the motel clerk. She said they were short, Hispanic, well-dressed, and driving a black Datsun."

"That's a radically different description," I said. "One of them is lying. Think it's worth dusting the motel room for prints?"

Jack gave me a sideways smile. "You'd be surprised how motels handle cleaning. We'd collect a couple hundred partials and still have nothing useful. But at least we've learned something, either the motel clerk or Ms. Johnson is lying."

"Okay," I said. "Where does that leave us?"

Jack rubbed his chin. "We need another angle. We haven't looked closely at the yacht that moved the night Jimmy was killed. The nearest vessel to Jimmy and the lobster pot with the treasure was Stillman's Sport Fisher. Its logbook claims it hasn't moved. But if Willy heard it running that night, it probably did. First thing tomorrow, let's visit Stillman."

"I'll meet you here at nine," I said.

I got home around seven that evening. Mother was sitting at the kitchen table, finishing dinner.

"How was your stroll with Jack?" she asked.

"It wasn't a stroll," I said. "We were questioning Vintner."

"I thought you didn't like Vintner."

"He's a fraud," I said. "And he might be a suspect."

"He seems successful. Drives a Mercedes," she said. "Have you considered dating him?"

"Never have and never will," I said flatly. "I'm not interested in living with someone unethical or living off someone else's money. I want my own."

She rolled her eyes in the way only a mother could, and I retreated to my room to reflect on the case and my life.

MORNING, WEDNESDAY, APRIL 15

The next morning, we drove in Jack's squad car to visit Stillman after Josie called ahead to confirm he'd be home. As we pulled into his estate, the scale of his personal power was hard to miss , sprawling grounds, sweeping ocean views, and a massive stone house in classic New England style.

We followed a long drive lined with blooming dogwoods before arriving at the front stoop, where a black-suited, gray-haired butler met us and ushered us through a wide entryway into a formal library. Walnut shelves lined the walls, packed with maritime artifacts and leather-bound volumes. The room reeked of wealth and cultivated taste.

Stillman sat behind a carved mahogany desk, its burgundy leather inlay gleaming in the morning light. He was chewing a toothpick, again.

"Chief. Judy," he said, removing the toothpick and dropping it in a nearby ashtray. "Trying to quit smoking. How are you both?"

"Fine," I said.

"A bit puzzled about recent events," Jack replied.

"How can I help?"

"Did your boat leave the marina two nights ago?" Jack asked.

"Not to my knowledge," Stillman said. "I haven't taken it out in weeks. Jimmy maintained the boat for me, or, I suppose, used to maintain it. He may have taken it out without asking. Did you check the onboard fuel log?"

"We did," Jack said. "It showed no recent activity."

"Then it likely didn't leave the dock. Jimmy was meticulous about records."

"Mind if I ask where you were that night?"

Stillman paused. "Let's see... I was at my salvage office in New Harbor until after ten. My staff can confirm that, if you're trying to eliminate me."

"When did you get home?"

"Midnight or so. My wife and the butler can vouch for that."

As Jack continued questioning, I wandered the room, taking in the artifacts. Stillman had spared no expense in curating his collection. A first-edition autobiography of an Arctic explorer. An ancient theodolite. A logbook from Darwin's *Beagle* voyage. These weren't knickknacks, they were serious acquisitions.

I realized that Stillman wasn't a trader. He was a collector. In my experience, buyers fell into three camps: decorators who wanted ambiance, flippers who wanted profit, and true collectors who acquired to preserve. Stillman was the third kind, obsessed, proud.

"You have some extraordinary pieces," I said.

"Thank you. The Maine Museum in Augusta has been pestering me for years to leave them the collection when I pass. Judy, I know you're in the business. If you ever encounter something rare, I'd appreciate a first crack at it."

The compliment came wrapped in a sting, he was dismissing my current inventory, flattering only my potential. I'd seen him exiting Vintner's shop more than once, parcels in hand. That bothered me. Vintner was a fraud. Stillman was the county's wealthiest collector.

I spotted a book titled *Antiquities Laws* on the corner of his desk. A folded slip marked a page. I picked it up out of curiosity. The author was Professor McIntyre from the University of Maine, a name I recognized. He was a trustee at the Maine Museum.

As I opened the front cover, Stillman moved beside me and, gently but firmly, took the book from my hands.

"Just a loan from a friend," he said.

But I'd already seen the inscription inside the cover.

It wasn't addressed to Stillman.

It was to Louie Vintner.

"Have you ever heard of Paulsgrave Williams?" I asked.

"William Paulsgrave?" Stillman replied, reversing the names. He was either stalling, dyslexic, or trying to appear confused. He looked down. People who are genuinely thinking tend to look up and away, not down. I sensed he was faking it.

"His name was Paulsgrave Williams, Jr.," I clarified.

"No, can't say that I have," he said. "Is he new in town?"

"No," I said evenly. "He was a pirate. Back in 1722."

"Really?" Stillman raised his brows. "I'm surprised the name doesn't ring a bell, then. Why do you ask?"

"There may be a connection to the case," Jack said, stepping in. "Anyway, we should be going. We've got another stop before the day's out."

He was cutting the conversation short. I wasn't sure why, but I followed his lead.

Once we walked back in the car, I asked, "Did I push too far, bringing up Paulsgrave?"

"No, that was a fair angle," Jack said. "I just don't want to tip our hand about the treasure. He might already know something, given his ties around town. But if he's involved, I'd rather he not know how much we know, not yet. Besides, only you and I have seen the goblet. Don, Randy, and Josie all know to keep their mouths shut."

"He knew about Jimmy," I said. "Think he could be connected?"

"I doubt it," Jack said. "He's got money, status, influence. A dozen well-placed friends. Why would he risk all that?"

"Maybe it's not about the money," I said. "Some collectors are compulsive. I've seen people who'll cross the line to complete a set. It borders on obsession."

Jack glanced sideways at me. "You've got Vintner on the brain again."

"That book on Stillman's desk, the one on antiquities law? It was inscribed to Vintner."

Jack stopped walking. "Seriously? Why didn't you say so?"

"Because I wasn't sure what it meant until now. But Stillman knows Vintner. And Vintner knows the state's leading expert on treasure law."

"Still doesn't connect them to murder," Jack said. "But good to know."

He climbed behind the wheel. "You know what? I will head to New Harbor and check on Stillman's alibi myself. Let's hold off talking to Vintner for now."

"While you're chasing alibis, I'll track down the professor."

"That's safe enough," Jack said. "Take good notes."

LATE AFTERNOON, WEDNESDAY, APRIL 15

The drive took me two hours to reach Orono, just north of Bangor, and another twenty minutes on foot, weaving through the University of Maine's campus buildings until I found the Natural Sciences building. I climbed creaky wooden stairs to the third floor and paused outside the office of Professor Allen McIntyre.

The door was open enough to reveal a cluttered cave of books, maps, and papers. Behind the pile sat a man who matched every ivory tower cliché: thin gray hair, half-round spectacles, a beige cardigan, and a Meerschaum pipe tucked beneath his chin.

"I hope you got the message I was coming," I said.

"Indeed. I rarely get visitors other than students. Please, come in."

"So, you're the university's expert on nautical antiquities?"

"A title reluctantly bestowed," he replied, with the ghost of a smile.

"I'm a dealer in nautical antiques from Boothbay Harbor," I said.

"I've heard of a few shops there," he replied coolly. "I haven't had reason to visit in years. Nautical antiquities are only one of my interests, but certainly a favorite. Since that's our shared focus, perhaps you'd like a private tour of our museum?"

"I'd love it," I said.

He led me down a long corridor and three flights of stairs into the basement. At the end of the hallway was a solid metal door. He tapped out a sequence on a keypad lock: six beeps and a click, then pushed open the heavy slab.

Flipping on the lights revealed a space nearly the size of three tennis courts. Cold fluorescent bulbs buzzed overhead. The room was dotted with glass display cases, each housing ancient nautical artifacts. Gold and silver gleamed in the nearest display like treasure from a conquistador's dream.

"Why does the university hide these treasures in a basement?" I asked.

"They're only here for study and will eventually be returned to the museums that loaned them," he said. "This room is the most secure one we have. It just happens to be in the basement."

"What do you learn from them?" I asked.

"Oh, collectively, they yield volumes of knowledge," he said. "Especially when we can find connections between them. For example, we learned that these two gold pieces in this display case came from the same tiny village in Colombia. They were cast back around when the officers from Christopher Columbus's three ships returned on their own to explore and, dare I say, plunder after Columbus's initial voyage and discoveries. From traces of rare minerals identified from analyzing microscopic samples and tool marks, and in rare cases, from similarities in design, we can even trace pieces back to a single unnamed artisan."

"Is that information useful?" I asked.

"Very," he said. "How else can we trace the early development of mankind if we don't preserve and study every ancient artifact we find? As scarce as they are, they serve as windows into our past."

"I've never considered antiquities in that light," I said. "I've only seen them for the prices they would bring in the marketplace."

"I understand," he said. "We both know their rareness drives collectors to offer high prices, which sadly has resulted in indispensable insight about our history being lost into the collectors' and even the black markets."

179

"Well, in my business, I rarely see pieces as old as these," I said.

"Rarely?" he asked. "Have you come across something significant?" His demeanor brightened considerably.

"Let's return to your office, so I can show you why I came to see you," I said.

On the way back, I told him about the murders and the treasure that had been discovered, carefully omitting any details that could compromise the investigation.

Back in his office, I settled into one of those uncomfortable wooden armchairs that universities use to prevent students from sitting too long. I reached into my oversized purse, where I had placed the goblet, carefully wrapped in bubble wrap, and nested inside a towel. I'd brought it directly from the shop's safe. I waited until the professor turned toward his bookshelf, then gently placed the goblet on his desk.

"Holy mackerel!" he cried, turning and catching sight of it. "What have you brought me?"

"Well, I'm sorry to say it's not for you," I said. "It's evidence in a murder case."

He opened his desk drawer, pulled out a slightly tarnished pair of white gloves, and slipped them on with ceremonial care. Then he gently lifted the goblet, rotating it like cradling a newborn.

"Has this find been reported to the state yet?" he asked.

"I don't think so," I said. "We believe this is only the tip of the iceberg. And truthfully, we're not sure how to notify the state. We don't want word getting out before we know what we're dealing with."

He turned to his bookshelf and pulled down a thick, well-used hardcover. He handed it to me.

Antiquities Laws of the State of Maine, by A.J. McIntyre.

"This will tell you how to report the find," he said, his tone more formal now. "You'd have violated the law if law enforcement weren't involved."

"You certainly must be familiar with Paulsgrave Williams," I said.

"Of course," he said. "Historical records place Paulsgrave Williams and his pirate crew near Boothbay Harbor in the early eighteenth century. Is this goblet connected with him?"

"According to an appraiser friend of mine, yes. He claims he has evidence linking the goblet to Edward English and then from him to Paulsgrave Williams."

"His full name was Paulsgrave Williams, Jr.," McIntyre added. "Delightful. I love the pirate period. If what you say is true, as an artifact, this goblet has extraordinary historical significance and inestimable value for understanding that era."

"And resale value," I said. "I hope one day to be the broker for its sale."

"Well, that may never come to pass for the portion that becomes the state's property, as required by law," he said. "And the state's portion is customarily the rarest object." Then he paused. "You know, it's funny…"

"That's not funny," I said, already anticipating trouble.

"Not funny in a comical way," he clarified. "Funny in a strange way. Three months ago, I came across an old treasure map stuck in the back of a ship's log. After careful study, I

181

concluded it was a fake, an early one, but fake, nonetheless. Now I'm wondering if it was more than that. In hindsight, it might've been a hand-drawn copy of the original map."

"What happened to it?" I asked, pulse rising.

"I gave it to one of the university's board members, along with an inscribed copy of that same book you're holding."

"Are you referring to Louie Vintner?" I asked.

"Why, yes," McIntyre said. "How did you possibly guess that?"

"I saw the copy of the book on Bernard Stillman's desk, inscribed to Vintner when we spoke with him yesterday. Vintner is my competitor, the other nautical antiquities dealer in Boothbay."

I could see the wheels turning in the professor's head.

"I wasn't aware Vintner was a dealer," he said. "Maybe Vintner sold the map to Stillman, allowing him to find Paulsgrave Williams's treasure. Or maybe they worked together on it."

"Stillman might have been involved, or he might know who was," I said. "Please don't discuss this with Vintner, Stillman, or anyone else until the murder investigation is over."

He nodded solemnly.

I returned the goblet to its wrappings and tucked it back into my purse, along with the book the professor had given me.

"You wouldn't want to leave that with me for the time being, would you?" he asked hopefully.

"Sorry," I said. "It's still evidence."

The professor stood and shook my hand.

As I opened his office door, I nearly collided with a trio of students preparing to knock. They stepped back and looked me up and down, trying to assess whether I was a professor, the professor's love interest, or perhaps just an ancient, meaning middle-aged, student.

I left them to their speculation.

"I'll be back in touch once we solve this mystery!" I called back as I turned down the hall and exited the building.

DUSK, WEDNESDAY APRIL 15

My brain was spinning by the time I reached my car. If Vintner had sold Stillman the map, then Stillman would have lied about everything. He might even know about the murders. He could be the killer if his motive was to conceal the treasure's discovery. But why hide it? Stillman had the resources to fight for legal ownership. Unless he didn't want it for money, he wanted it for possession. Stillman wasn't interested in resale value or public admiration. He was a collector, obsessive. He didn't care about historical significance, only that it was his. The goblet in my purse might still be the missing piece he craved.

But what if Vintner hadn't told him about the map? Maybe Vintner was working alone. My gut said Vintner wouldn't have the guts to kill anyone, but he might hire someone who would. We knew he was linked to the two suspicious men at the motel. Maybe he hired them. Or perhaps he partnered with Stillman to split the treasure.

Then, another thought struck me. If Stillman didn't have the whole collection, he'd want the goblet. That goblet might be the bait we needed.

183

Excited, I jumped in my car and sped toward Jack's office. As the sun dropped behind the tree line, I turned off Route 1 onto Route 27.

That's when I noticed a vehicle riding my bumper.

At first, I was annoyed, then alert. It was a red Toyota pickup.

The motel clerk had described the same make and color.

I accelerated. It stayed with me. Then it pulled alongside, holding even in the opposing lane. I glanced over. The windows were tinted too dark to make out the driver. As it looked like the truck might swerve into me, headlights appeared behind us, another car. The truck hesitated, then surged forward and disappeared down the road.

I kept the second car near me, hoping it would stay close. I followed the truck as far as I could, but it vanished a few turns later, as did the other vehicle.

By the time I reached the harbor, I was alone again, physically and mentally shaken.

I parked in front of my shop, then crossed the street to Jack's office.

He was back from checking Stillman's alibi. I told him everything.

"Well, it's probably gone for now," Jack said. "Since you could not catch any part of the license number, there's nothing more we can do now."

I paced back and forth, still shaken by the red truck and fueled by adrenaline. I jabbered at Jack about the meeting with the professor, the inscribed book, and what Stillman might be hiding.

"Well, Stillman's alibi was confirmed by two ladies at his boatyard office and a guy at his warehouse," Jack said. "I also stopped by his estate again. His wife and the butler both corroborated his story."

"People whose loyalty he owns," I countered.

"True," Jack agreed. "But one possible clue came from the guy at the warehouse. His southern accent and your red Toyota truck line up with what the motel clerk told Don and Randy."

As we talked, I kept moving, either from nerves or the buzz of finally closing in on the truth.

"Vintner knows the professor," I said. "Stillman knows Vintner, who knew who Paulsgrave Williams was, even though he denied it. Stillman had Vintner's book. If Vintner sold him the professor's map, then one or both are involved in the treasure, and possibly the murders."

"I still have trouble picturing Stillman pulling a trigger," Jack said. "But maybe the two motel guys did."

"Maybe Stillman hired them," I said.

"Or maybe they worked for Vintner, who was trying to retrieve the treasure himself," Jack said. "Either way, both men had the means and motive. Vintner's card was found at the motel. He could've hired those two to find the treasure or steal it back from Stillman. And if that's true, Stillman's life might be in danger."

As we spoke, Josie was pounding away on her computer. I assumed she was entering report information, but she had been running a name and address search.

"Jeanine Johnson has a nephew who uses the moniker Cracker Johnson. His full name is Chester Johnson. He spent two stints in Thomaston State Prison, one for aggravated assault and battery, for five years, and another two for safe-cracking. He also has juvenile records for auto theft, petty theft, and drunk and disorderly."

"A tough guy," I said.

"Any word on known associates?" Jack asked.

"Only a possible, his cellmate, who was released the same day Cracker was, about a year back," Josie said. "Richard O'Neill, Jr. His nickname is Junior."

"Either name line up with the southern guy at the warehouse?" I asked.

Jack pulled out his notebook and started flipping through it.

"You know, I think I wrote down the guy's name at the warehouse, but I don't recollect what it was or for certain that I noted it," Jack said. "Man, that'd be sloppy police work if I didn't."

I thought, "Well, the man is human; maybe he can make a mistake." Jack kept flipping pages back and forth, looking for the name among his notes.

"So she has the same last name as her nephew. That's why the 7-Eleven clerk accepted the credit card, the name on the card matched Cracker's driver's license," I said. "And she knows Cracker well enough to give him her credit card."

"Not because she expects him to return it," Jack said. "She'll almost certainly report it being stolen after he leaves town, so she doesn't have to pay his expenses."

"We might be getting somewhere," I said. We can be fairly certain the description the woman gave is phony, a cover-up for her nephew. The odds are even better that the motel manager's description is right. So, we know their names, description, and vehicle."

"And we might know where they are, assuming the guy I interviewed is Junior O'Neill," Jack said. "However, we know nothing of how they might be linked to the murder or the treasure."

"Aren't crimes most frequently solved in the first forty-eight hours, before leads turn cold?" Josie asked.

"Don't remind me," Jack said.

"We're more than seventy-two hours into this one," I said.

"I said don't remind me," Jack said with a smile.

Jack was still flipping back and forth in his notebook. Don and Randy walked in and found chairs.

"Here it is," Jack said. "Dick O'Neill, short for Richard O'Neill, aka Junior O'Neill, was the guy who provided Stillman's alibi over at his warehouse in New Harbor."

"Now the game's afoot," I said. "Let's request a search warrant for Stillman's house."

"Whoa," Jack said. "We don't have a shred of physical evidence, no connection between Johnson and O'Neill and any crime, no connection between O'Neill and Johnson beyond their time in prison, or between either of them and Stillman, except possibly working for him. And we have no connection between Stillman and any crime. All we have is the possibility Stillman lied if Vintner sold him the map. Besides, Judge Patrick happens to be Stillman's golfing buddy, and they both sit on the board of the only bank in town. There is no way he will bend the requirements for probable cause. Finally, the two men and Vintner have a vague business card connection. We might ask the motel clerk to ID them, but we have no cause to round them up for a line-up."

"What about Vintner?" I asked. "He's connected to Stillman by the book. Could we get a warrant for his phone records?"

"And what would that prove?" Jack asked. "That he knows Stillman? That Stillman's a customer? We already know that. We are nowhere."

"Maybe we could sweat it out of him," I said.

"You are competitive, aren't you?" Jack said.

"Maybe we should interview him, at least."

"We have to be careful," Jack said, turning to Don and Randy. "That could tip him off. If they're involved, they probably think they've stumped us. Do you guys have anything new?"

"We got nothin'," Don said.

"So, if Vintner finds out we're suspicious, he could warn Stillman, if they're both involved, and Stillman will firm up his alibi and bury any evidence," I said.

"You got it," Jack said. "You'll have to live with your competitive angst a little longer."

It was growing late. We sat in silence for a while. Then Josie left for home. Randy followed. Finally, Don. Jack and I were alone in the office, the overhead lights buzzing softly.

Jack sat behind his desk, and I was kicked back in one of his side chairs.

"You know what?" I said. "After talking with Professor McIntyre, I realized my dreams of wealth might not be the best life strategy. Maybe other priorities should matter more."

"Really?" Jack asked, arching an eyebrow.

"Seeing Stillman and all that wealth, more than he could ever appreciate, I started to understand that accumulating treasure isn't as fulfilling as learning about its history. The joy I get from my business isn't about making a profit. It's about discovering the stories behind the objects. When I spoke with McIntyre, I saw how much knowledge can come from items I've only seen as inventory. I realized I've been on the wrong train, not just the wrong track."

"Sounds like a healthy revelation," Jack said.

"Hey," I added. "On my way back from the professor, before the red truck encounter, I had an idea. If greed drives Stillman, maybe we can use that greed to trap him. Or if Vintner's the mastermind, it might flush him out."

"Or someone else entirely," Jack said. "How would it work?"

"We use the goblet and the other treasure as bait."

"I don't see how that'll do it," Jack said. "The killer, or killers, might already feel satisfied with their haul."

"Somebody killed for it," I said. "Even if Jimmy's murder was revenge for taking a part of the loot, I think he might've kept the best piece, the goblet. That makes it the most tempting thing we've got."

Jack had me doubting my thinking. My brain kicked into overdrive and birthed another idea.

"I know what we can do," I said. "Let's create more; make it look like we found an additional stash of treasure near where the first one was discovered."

"What additional treasure?" Jack asked.

"We'll fake it. We'll create the illusion of more treasure, another batch missed by the original hunters."

"Even if that worked, how would we leak the word out?"

189

"Vintner," I said. "That way, we'll find out if the person involved is Vintner, Stillman, both, or neither."

Jack grew interested, popped out of his chair, and started pacing.

"Now I get it," he said. "You slip the word to Vintner; he tells Stillman, if Stillman's involved, and we... Wait. What happens next?"

"We wait," I said. "I'll let Vintner know the additional treasure is in my safe. We'll watch from the building across from my office. If either of them wants it badly enough, they'll come at night to break in. Whoever cares will come themselves or send Cracker Johnson with his safe-cracking skills, probably with Junior O'Neill for backup."

"Whoever shows up gets arrested," Jack said.

"If I act casually, Vintner won't suspect a thing."

"It's probably worth a shot since we've got nothin' else goin'," Jack said. "I don't see how it could hurt. I hope you're a good actress."

"My brain's in overdrive. I've got an old chest in my attic that nobody knows I have," I said. "It's not too big and looks like a treasure chest. Might even have been one."

"I'll send Don and Randy back out to the island after Vintner opens shop in the morning," Jack said. "I'll stow the chest on the launch tonight, under cover of dark, so no one sees it."

"Vintner listens in on your radio transmissions," I reminded him.

"Right," Jack nodded. "In the morning, I'll create radio chatter about their mission. On the way back, they'll report finding something. I'll have Don and Randy return with the chest by noon. They'll carry it up the street, loaded with rocks so it looks heavy, and bring it into your office."

"Yes," I said. "Then we transfer the rocks into the safe and leave the empty chest beside it. Vintner will see the whole operation except for the rock swap. You'll have to distract him while Don and I do that. I'll even let him peek at the real goblet to seal the illusion."

"An elaborate plan," Jack said. "It might just work. I'll tell Don to rub dirt on the chest, so it looks like it came straight from underground."

I went home to retrieve the chest from the attic. Mother helped me lower it down.

The chest was ornate, about three feet long, a foot and a half tall, and about as wide.

"You starting a hope chest?" she asked, half in jest.

"Let's just say I hope it will lead to a revelation," I said.

She gave me that all-knowing, snarky smile that only mothers can manage.

I waited impatiently until dark before sneaking out to deliver the chest to Jack. I went south, away from the street where our shops were, and around the other way to Jack's office.

NIGHT, WEDNESDAY APRIL 16

Well, after darkness had settled in the harbor and the shops had gone dark, Jack and I met Don and Randy at the police launch. Jack had already told Don about the plan. He handed the chest to Randy, who stowed it below deck.

"Here, take this burlap sack, too," Jack told Don. "I've included a dozen small rocks in case you don't find enough loose ones to fill the chest or pack around the larger ones. If you can fill the chest completely with rocks you find there, then bring this bag back like additional treasure."

We heard a faint sound as we were sneaking back from the launch.

"Pssst," Mr. Parker hissed from his rocker on his porch. "I can see you're up to something sneaky, but mum's the word."

Jack just gave him a smile and a silent wave. I hoped that he wasn't somehow involved.

Back at the office, we reviewed the plan. Everyone knew Vintner routinely closed his shop for lunch around 1:00 p.m. for an hour. Jack would call Don on the radio in the morning when Vintner would likely listen to his scanner. Jack would broadcast that Don and Randy's mission was to look for evidence on the island because they were stumped on the investigation.

Then, on the way back, Don would radio Jack and report that they had uncovered a treasure chest full of pirate loot.

Finally, to ensure Vintner saw the additional treasure, the deputies would carry the chest up the street, past his shop to mine, as soon as they saw him return from lunch. Josie would watch for his return, and when Vintner was sitting at his desk, signal the deputies with a sign, stroking her hair.

The next day, Don and Randy returned on schedule. They radioed ahead, reporting they had discovered a significant stash of pirate treasure and asking Jack to meet them to assist with the load. Jack responded that they would store it in my safe until they could turn it over to the state in a day or two.

When the launch docked, Don, Randy, and Jack unloaded the chest and the burlap bag onto the dock. Don also handed Jack a plastic evidence bag.

"It's a toothpick," Don said. "We found it at the scene."

"This won't change our immediate strategy, but it might help the case in the future if we find DNA on it," Jack said, pocketing the baggie.

Don handed Jack the same burlap sack he'd been given. Then he and Randy began carrying the chest down the street, waddling along, stopping to rest several times. It took both deputies' full strength to carry the rock-filled chest. Thank goodness it was sturdy. As instructed, they carried it past Vintner's shop and into mine, with Jack following close behind with the sack.

I removed the goblet and set it in plain view atop the safe while we hid the transfer of the rocks. No one saw. We left the empty chest and the burlap sack beside the safe to give the impression the treasure had all been stashed.

As expected, Vintner appeared at my window just in time to see me grab the goblet, as if it were the last piece of a vast treasure and swiftly tuck it inside the safe as if trying to hide it. I locked the safe with a dramatic flourish just before

Jack and I walked out of the shop, passing Vintner. He fell in behind us, pretending to be heading back to his store, but he kept just within earshot.

"You'd better call that Boston appraiser friend of yours and see if he can come up tomorrow to evaluate this accumulation of treasure," Jack said loudly enough for the next block to hear. "Ask him to stay a couple of days."

"I'll do that right away," I said. "I don't want to keep such valuable pieces in my safe longer than necessary."

I caught Vintner in my peripheral vision as he entered his shop. I figured he'd be on the phone within minutes, to Stillman, the two ruffians, or someone else in the scheme.

Jack, Don, Randy, and I returned to his office.

"Don, I want you to start walking a patrol past Judy's office once an hour, on the hour," Jack said. "Maintain strict regularity, so Vintner will see how predictable it is. When it turns dark, the rest of you should make it appear you're headed home. After about an hour, I'll leave by the back door of my office and meet up with the rest of you. You can sneak back via the alley to the building across from Judy's shop. I've arranged to leave the back door open with the lady who owns the building. Go up to the second floor, to the room in the center of the building. From the windows of that room, we should have an unimpeded view of the only door to Judy's office, where we'll be able to see anyone breaking in. The windows in the second-floor room have Venetian blinds that will disguise our presence yet still leave small openings through which we can watch without being seen."

We broke up like a football huddle.

I went home, knowing I could sneak back unseen through the alley from its north end to the back of the building, as Jack had directed.

When I came in, my mother was knitting in her rocking chair.

"Glad to see you home early," she said. "Maybe we can sit down to a meal together for a change."

"Can't tonight," I said. "Don't wait up for me. I'll be on an all-night stakeout."

"Is that what they call it nowadays?" she asked.

Fully aware of her insinuation, I chose not to respond. "The case I'm working on with Jack could be resolved in the next day or two."

"All's well that ends well," she said.

When night had settled on our quiet little town, dressed in dark clothing, I sneaked out and down the alley.

AFTER DARK, THURSDAY APRIL 16

We assembled in the center room on the second floor according to plan. Jack, Randy, and I waited in the dark, watching to see who might arrive at my shop, maybe the two men from the motel, maybe Vintner, maybe Stillman himself, or perhaps someone completely unknown. Or no one at all.

We peered through tiny gaps in the venetian blinds. The street below was quiet and open, most of the parked cars gone for the night. We had a clear view of the shop's entrance, but the safe was out of sight, hidden behind the dense display of my merchandise. That bothered me slightly, though not enough to derail the plan. The only way in or out was through the front door, and we had that covered.

195

Don waited downstairs. At the top of each hour, he exited our building's back door, entered the rear of Jack's office, and then walked out the front to conduct his visible patrol. He looped back, slipped into our building again, and took position near the front door, ready to rush out on Jack's signal if anything happened.

MIDNIGHT TO DAWN, FRIDAY APRIL 17

The night dragged on. Midnight crept to 2:00 a.m., then 4:00. Finally, a pink glow began to stir on the horizon.

"Looks like your plan didn't work," Jack said softly.

"I believed it had a fair shot," I said, disappointed. "Maybe my intuition about what would tempt them was wrong."

We quietly filed downstairs and out onto the street. I headed to my shop. Jack, Randy, and Don turned toward their office.

As I unlocked my front door, I let out a yell.

Jack, Randy, and Don came sprinting back. They were beside me in seconds, gawking at the empty space where my safe had stood.

Behind where the safe had been a jagged hole, a foot wider and taller than the safe itself, sliced clean through the shared wall with the fish store next door.

We had never imagined they might come through the wall.

"How could they possibly have taken the safe through the wall?" I asked, stunned.

"A heavy hand truck did the trick," Jack said. "See how the wheels crushed the remaining wallboard near the floor and left gouges in your floor beyond? I'll see where they went out."

Jack stepped over the debris and ducked through the hole to the other side. I stood in shock, the smell of the fish shop wafting through the breach.

Jack returned ten minutes later.

"Whoever they were, they took the safe to the fish shop's loading dock. A truck could've easily approached from the back, where we wouldn't have seen it."

"Not only did we not catch the culprits, we lost the goblet and the coins," I said.

"And the rocks," Randy added.

Jack smiled sheepishly.

"Well, Judy, you're partly right," he said.

"What?" I asked, blinking at him.

"One of the rocks you put in the safe was fake. I hid a miniature but powerful radio transmitter inside it, so the situation might not be a total loss."

"What?" I repeated. "Why did you even think to do that? And why didn't you tell me?"

"It was a basic backup plan," Jack said. "A technique I picked up in Special Forces. I tucked it into the burlap sack with the spare rocks."

"Good thing we brought the burlap sack back," Don said.

"Special Forces?" I asked. "You never, "

"Once they open the safe to remove the goblet, we should be able to pick up the signal," Jack said.

197

"From how far away?" I asked. "They could be in another state before they open it."

Just then, Josie burst through the front door.

"I pulled the mugshots of Cracker Johnson and his cellmate from the prison records," she said, breathless. "They're both assigned to the parole office in New Harbor."

"Let me see those," Jack said. He studied the photos. "Yes. The shorter one is the guy I saw working at Stillman's warehouse. That's our best bet for where the safe is headed."

"If it isn't already there," I said.

"Josie, notify New Harbor's police chief, Harry Horton," Jack said quickly. "Ask him to meet us at Stillman's marine salvage warehouse but to wait out of sight until we arrive. Then call the State Police and tell them to send backup. And call Judge Wilson over in New Harbor for a warrant. Don't call Judge Patrick here, Stillman's too well connected. Ask Judge Wilson to call Chief Horton when the warrant is ready so he can pick it up on his way."

Jack and I ran for his squad car. Don and Randy sprinted for theirs. Josie turned and darted back toward the office.

We sped toward New Harbor, hoping to catch up with the thieves, the treasure, and the suspected murderers.

EARLY MORNING, FRIDAY APRIL 17

The sun was fully up by the time we reached the warehouse. It was still early, just after six-thirty. The area was zoned marine industrial, with no residential housing in sight.

198

The side streets were deserted, and the building looked lifeless. I feared I'd guessed wrong again.

We located New Harbor's police chief, Harry Horton, a pot-bellied, middle-aged man with bulging forearms like Popeye. He sat waiting around the corner in his squad car. We pulled up beside him, and I rolled down my window so Jack could speak across me.

"Harry, any sign of movement?" Jack asked.

"Nothing since I arrived," Harry said. "Hi, Judy."

I knew Harry through the Boothbay Harbor Rotary Club. Our clubs co-hosted a joint fundraiser each spring. I gave him a silent wave.

"No sign of the troopers yet?" Jack asked. "Don, check for the tracking signal."

"The troopers just radioed; they'll be here in about twenty minutes," Harry replied.

"Sorry, boss," Don said, fiddling with the handheld tracker. "No signal."

"We can't wait," Jack said. "They could be melting it down."

"Let's go," I said, adrenaline bubbling.

"Not so fast," Jack said, turning to me. "You've been helpful, but this could get dangerous. You have to stay here. Besides, we need someone to brief the troopers when they arrive, tell them where we went, and how many of us are inside."

I was miffed but didn't fight the inevitable. Jack and Harry, with Don and Randy close behind, moved toward a side

199

door just to the right of a twelve-foot roll-up. Don carried a crowbar.

The door was solid and locked, but it gave way quietly. I stood by the car long enough for Jack to glance back and confirm I was staying put, and then I followed. I wasn't about to miss this.

When I reached the door, they were moving in single file through a dark bay with high ceilings, heading toward a lit office in the back. Through its cloudy windows, I saw four people hunched over a table, their backs to us.

They didn't see it coming. when Jack and the others burst through the office door.

I slipped in behind them. Stillman jumped to his feet, hands raised. Cracker Johnson and Junior O'Neill moved instinctively into fighting stances. Cracker had a cutting torch lit in his right hand. He shifted it to his left, his right hand moving toward a revolver tucked in his waistband.

But he stopped.

With four guns aimed at him, he thought better of it. He switched off the torch. Don quickly disarmed him. Randy snapped the cuffs on Junior O'Neill. I noted Cracker's revolver was equipped with a silencer.

The real shock came next.

The fourth person in the room, the one none of us expected, was Bonnie Martin.

She clung to Stillman's arm like she'd been there for months. Her presence cast new light on Bill Martin's murder. Maybe it hadn't been about poaching or treasure after all.

Then came shouting and boots. Four state troopers stormed in, two of them dragging Vintner by the arms.

"We found this guy sneaking out the back as we came in," one said.

"I was just on my way back from the head," Vintner muttered.

Jack stepped forward. "So, you haven't touched the safe?"

"No, like I said, I just arrived here," Stillman replied.

"Then you won't object to us checking your hands with the ultraviolet light we brought?" Jack asked. "You see, I treated the safe with an invisible silky powder that's hard to wash off. It's only visible under ultraviolet light."

Stillman looked at Jack with fury in his eyes.

"You bastard," he said. "And I thought you were too stupid to figure out who was involved."

"Well, not as stupid as the guy who just fell for Jack's malarkey about ultraviolet powder," I said.

Stillman exploded, actually growling aloud. Being outsmarted by someone he considered ignorant was bad enough, being mocked by a woman he saw as his inferior in all things antiquities was worse.

"Jack, here's the warrant you ordered," Harry said, stepping into the doorway.

Jack unfolded it and gave it a quick scan. "Very good. Josie even included your house, Stillman. It's time we do a little treasure hunting of our own. Lock them all up, Harry. We'll sort them out after we investigate further."

"No problem," Harry said.

When we searched Stillman's house, we found a secret room that reminded me of the 1950s movie *King Solomon's Mines*, a cavern of gold and stolen glory. Paulsgrave Williams Jr.'s treasure was in the center of Stillman's hoard. His original chest had collapsed under the weight of its contents, spilling coins across the floor like a glistening, frozen waterfall. Other gold and silver artifacts crowded shelves and cases, many later identified as stolen from museums and private collections worldwide. Jack arranged for them to be returned, but not before Professor McIntyre had time to study them thoroughly.

The sight of it all, the lost history, the secrets held in metal and wood, reminded me of what really matters. The artifacts weren't just relics of wealth. They were stories, identities, and windows into lost civilizations. Maybe Stillman, without meaning to, had done the world a service by keeping them together.

Eventually, Junior O'Neill turned on Cracker Johnson. Cracker, in turn, fingered Stillman as the mastermind. Stillman implicated Vintner as his pipeline to the underground market. They proved the adage: there's no honor among thieves. Bonnie Martin, it turned out, was guilty only of falling for the wrong man. She hadn't known anything.

As it came out, Jimmy had been captaining Stillman's boat while Cracker and Junior ferried treasure from the hole. On one trip back, Jimmy decided to skim a portion for himself, stashing it inside one of Bill Martin's lobster traps. He probably intended to retrieve it later.

But as fate would have it, Bill spotted Jimmy pulling a trap and thought he was poaching. He pulled a shotgun and prepared to call it in. That's when Cracker returned. Seeing

Jimmy held at gunpoint, he shot Bill, claiming he was protecting his accomplice. In the confusion, Jimmy secured the trap to the boat's seaward side, hoping it would go unnoticed when they docked.

Later, Cracker and the others took Bill's body, buried it in the hole they'd dug the treasure from, and scuttled his boat with a blast from his shotgun. Jimmy cut the trap free once back at the harbor, intending to return for it, never realizing it would be his undoing.

Stillman eventually discovered the goblet missing. Cracker returned to retrieve it from Jimmy, but when Jimmy resisted, Cracker shot him with a .38 fitted with a silencer. Jack would later prove it was the same gun that killed Jimmy.

Stillman's wife was charged as an accessory after the fact, though she'd tried to preserve the collection, forbidding him from melting down the coins or selling them to unscrupulous buyers. She began divorce proceedings the moment she learned about Bonnie Martin.

Jack also found a journal hidden behind a wall panel detailing illicit antiquities transactions. The journal named a half-dozen major buyers, including Judge Patrick and several city councilmen. That would be a storm for another day.

With Jack's blessing, I called Rodney to oversee the treasure's appraisal and help Professor McIntyre catalog and study everything. Together, they would determine which pieces belonged to the state and could be returned to museums and rightful owners. A month ago, I would've cared a lot more about what I could've earned from that treasure.

Now? Not so much.

What mattered most to me wasn't what those coins were worth. It was what they meant, what they taught. And maybe what they revealed about the kind of person I wanted to be.

As I stood on the dock that evening, watching the police launch glide across the darkening harbor, Jack stepped up beside me.

"You still dreaming about buried treasure?" he asked.

I smiled. "Not the kind you can lock in a safe."

Jack nodded slowly, looking out at the fading horizon.

"Maybe," he said, nudging my shoulder gently, "you and I could start chasing stories together, instead of treasure."

I raised an eyebrow. "Is that your idea of a date?"

"Depends. You like chowder?"

I grinned. "Only if you're buying."

He grinned. "Deal. And maybe... next Saturday too?"

I smiled. "We'll see if you behave."

And just like that, I realized some treasures aren't gold or silver. Some treasures are flesh and blood. And maybe, just maybe, some stories are only beginnings.

Find other books by Charles Patton at
charlespattonbooks.com

www.ingramcontent.com/pod-product-compliance
Lightning Source LLC
Chambersburg PA
CBHW020954180626
46814CB00003B/1087